SMOKE AND SHADOW

DON'T MISS THESE OTHER THRILLING STORIES IN THE WORLDS OF

HALO

Halo: Retribution
Troy Denning

Halo: Envoy
Tobias S. Buckell

Halo: Smoke and Shadow
Kelly Gay

Halo: Fractures: More Essential Tales of the Halo Universe
(anthology)

Halo: Shadow of Intent
Joseph Staten

Halo: Last Light
Troy Denning

Halo: Saint's Testimony
Frank O'Connor

Halo: Hunters in the Dark
Peter David

Halo: New Blood
Matt Forbeck

Halo: Broken Circle
John Shirley

THE KILO-FIVE TRILOGY

Karen Traviss

Halo: Glasslands

Halo: The Thursday War

Halo: Mortal Dictata

THE FORERUNNER SAGA

Greg Bear

Halo: Cryptum

Halo: Primordium

Halo: Silentium

Halo: Evolutions: Essential Tales of the Halo Universe (anthology)

Halo: The Cole Protocol
Tobias S. Buckell

Halo: Contact Harvest
Joseph Staten

Halo: Ghosts of Onyx
Eric Nylund

Halo: First Strike
Eric Nylund

Halo: The Flood
William C. Dietz

Halo: The Fall of Reach
Eric Nylund

HALO

SMOKE AND SHADOW

KELLY GAY

BASED ON THE BESTSELLING VIDEO GAME FOR XBOX®

GALLERY BOOKS
New York   London   Toronto   Sydney   New Delhi

G

Gallery Books
An Imprint of Simon & Schuster, Inc.
1230 Avenue of the Americas
New York, NY 10020

Copyright © 2016 by Microsoft Corporation. All rights reserved.

Microsoft, Halo, the Halo logo, Xbox, and the Xbox logo are trademarks of the Microsoft group of companies.

"Into the Fire" was originally published in the collection *Halo: Fractures* copyright © 2016 by Microsoft Corporation.

First Gallery Books trade paperback edition January 2018

GALLERY BOOKS and colophon are registered trademarks of Simon & Schuster, Inc.

For information about special discounts for bulk purchases, please contact Simon & Schuster Special Sales at 1-866-506-1949 or business@simonandschuster.com.

The Simon & Schuster Speakers Bureau can bring authors to your live event. For more information or to book an event contact the Simon & Schuster Speakers Bureau at 1-866-248-3049 or visit our website at www.simonspeakers.com.

Manufactured in the United States of America

10 9 8 7 6 5 4 3 2 1

Library of Congress Cataloging-in-Publication Data is available.

ISBN 978-1-5011-5540-6
ISBN 978-1-5011-4460-8 (ebook)

PART ONE

INTO THE FIRE

ONE

Today, she sold weapons to a hinge-head.

The small lot of spikers and carbines would keep her crew happy, her ship operational, and her informants eager for a piece of the pie.

It was a lovely little circle of profit she'd created for herself.

And Rion loved it. She was *good* at it. She'd forged her way to success and never hesitated to fight bare-knuckled to stay there. She was proud to call herself one of New Tyne's most notable salvagers.

But success wasn't all golden.

There were some sales, some transactions that left dark smudges somewhere deep inside her, where things like honor and integrity and loyalty lurked. Dark karmic tally marks that put a few kinks in that lovely little circle.

Every time one of her lots sold to ex-Covenant, the nagging sense of betrayal didn't let up until she hiked herself down to Stavros's and had a few drinks. Her crew thought it was simply a ritual, a small way to celebrate yet another payday, another sign that their jobs were secure and going strong. But inside, behind the jokes and the smiles and the laughter, a sour taste lingered in Rion's throat.

She wondered what he'd say if he knew, if he could see her now. Daddy's little girl all grown up and on the wrong side of the law.

Though, these days, there wasn't much law to be found.

And sides? In postwar, there were plenty of those to go around.

Rion's side, or lack thereof, was neutrality. Her business depended on it. She stayed out of politics, religions, and rebellions. There was a time her family would have said that staying neutral was just as bad as choosing the wrong side. But times had changed and family was just a memory.

"All set," she said as the bank confirmation appeared on her commpad.

"Always a pleasure, Captain. Not as good as last month, but respectable."

The prior month had been one of Rion's best paydays ever, a four-way bidding war for a small piece of Forerunner nav tech that she'd come across by chance in a small bazaar on Komoya, one of Vitalyevna's moons. The databoard was damaged and the crystal chip smashed, but it hadn't seemed to matter. Forerunner tech and relics were *always* a hot commodity. Intel was hard to come by, so Rion spent much of her downtime digging in files and researching in places she shouldn't be just to learn more about the ancient race.

And then she'd found intel on her ticket to retirement—a device called a luminary, which would supposedly point the way to all sorts of interesting Forerunner salvage. . . .

Rion reached into her pocket, grabbed the flex card she'd put there, broke it in half, and placed the bright orange equivalent of two hundred fifty credits on the desk.

Nor Fel glanced at the amount stamped on the surface, then lifted her large avian head. Clear membranes swept horizontally across her yellow eyes, the Kig-Yar version of a blink. She cocked her head, the tendons and muscles above her eyes pulling together into consideration.

Nor placed the tip of her claw on the card, holding it there while she gazed at Rion, and then cackled. "I knew you'd bite."

Despite their obvious differences, Rion and Nor understood each other and enjoyed a mutually beneficial relationship. Devious and cunning, Nor possessed a greed that was only exceeded by the high regard in which she held herself and her T'vaoan lineage. She was an excellent strategist and knew that relations and good business were the key to keeping the money flowing. And the money was *always* flowing.

After Nor's mate, Sav Fel, disappeared four years ago, Nor had created an empire on Venezia, a clearinghouse of postwar scrap and surplus. Salvagers brought in their goods; the clearinghouse catalogued them and took a percentage; and come the first day of every Venezian month, the items went up for auction—everything from Titanium-A plating and molecular memory circuits to small arms and transport vessels. Nor ruled over her house with an iron claw and a set of craftily devised rules that everyone—salvager and buyer alike—abided by.

Her clients included those from the industrial, tech, medical, and manufacturing sectors, along with ex-Covenant, fringe and religious groups, rebels of one faction or another, and independent government militias. She was on the radar of every military group out there—Rion figured she was on a few herself—but mostly Nor's clearinghouse was left alone. One, because this was Venezia, and Venezia played by its own rules. And two, because Nor refused to move heavy ordnance of any kind. Rumor had it that her mate had gotten mixed up in trafficking something big and it had cost him.

"They will not be happy, your crew." Nor nodded toward the window, where Lessa and the new hire, Kip, waited outside by the truck, talking. "With the payday you just made, one would think a break is in order. I hear Sundown is nice this time of year."

"Sundown is nice any time of year." Which Nor knew full well. "Breaks aren't really my thing, Nor. Just ask my crew." And they also wouldn't be happy to learn that Rion was about to use a good portion of their payday on the next operation. "Word's floating around about big scrap in one of the border systems." Rion gestured to the flex card on the desk. "Haven't sold my info away, have you?"

Nor's high-pitched squawk grated over Rion's eardrums, making her wince.

"You know I keep my word," Nor said. "Me and you, we have an agreement, yes? Have I ever broken it?"

"Nope, can't say that you have."

The small downy feathers on the back of Nor's head ruffled, indicating she was incredibly proud and satisfied by the admission.

Rion couldn't fault Nor for preening; her information was always good. The old bird had informants across the entire Via Casilina Trade Route that had arisen between the Qab, Cordoba,

Shaps, Elduros, and Sverdlosk systems. In the past, Rion had been forced to wait for other salvagers to fail to deliver before Nor would then resell her precious intel at a more affordable price. When Rion kept returning successful when no one else was, her reputation and her bank account grew, and so had her business relationship with Nor.

Nor opened a desk drawer and pushed the flex card inside. "It's not my information . . . but for this price, I send you to the one who possesses it. He is expecting you, I am sure. Get to it quick and you might end up rich as me. One day." Her beak clicked together as she gave a raspy chuckle. "But remember my rules, yes? No trouble."

Now *that* was interesting. The familiar zing of possibility ran through Rion's veins. Had to be something controversial, something big. Military, probably. *Trouble* to Nor meant heavy ordnance. And where there was heavy ordnance, there was usually a wealth of tech and surplus.

Paranoid as usual, Nor didn't say the name aloud, but rather legibly scratched it onto a piece of paper with her claw, then handed it over.

Rion read the scratch and lifted her brow. "Really?"

Nor shrugged.

"This'd better be worth it."

A chilly breeze tossed Rion's dark hair around her face as she headed for the truck. Gray clouds hovered over New Tyne's center. The soft glow of city lights emerging as day gave way to night was so warm and inviting that it almost made her long for a place with roots and a simpler life. *Almost.*

"So?" Lessa pushed away from the hood of the truck with a heavy shiver in her voice. "How was the old bird today?"

Rion shook her head at her young crewmember. "Next time, wear a jacket, Less. Or wait *inside* the truck. Long winter might be over, but those thin fatigues won't cut it for a few more months yet."

"I draw the line at six months of winter fatigues. Besides, we hardly stay long enough for the weather to matter much." Lessa ducked into the passenger seat.

Lessa hadn't met a human or an alien she couldn't or wouldn't talk to. She was blessed with a friendly face, a beguiling smile, and a mop of tight blonde curls that never stayed tucked into her braid for very long. Out of necessity, the young woman had learned early on how to read people and use her looks and personality to their fullest advantage. While Lessa was charming the pants off an unlucky target, her younger brother, Niko, was somewhere nearby hacking into the target's commpad. They made quite a team. And when they'd targeted Rion two years ago in the mining slums of Aleria, rather than turn them over to the local authorities, Rion had offered them a job. One of the smarter decisions she'd made in recent years.

"So, payday was good, then?" Lessa began fiddling with the heater as Kip squeezed his well-built frame into the backseat.

Rion started the truck. "Yeah, it was good. Just one more stop before we head back." She pulled out of the lot and then eased into traffic, wondering how to break the news. They'd been out six weeks on their last job, only returning today. The guys back at the ship had just unloaded a *very* nice stasis field generator for Nor's pickup crew. The last thing on their minds was jumping systems again.

In the silence, Rion could feel Lessa's lengthy stare and knew what was coming.

"Please tell me you didn't." Rion's wince affirmed Lessa's suspicions. "Aw, great. Just great. You *promised* us some offship R and R."

"It's just intel, Less. It doesn't mean we have to take off right away."

Lessa folded her arms over her chest and slumped in her seat. She blew a strand of hair from her face with a huff, and then suddenly turned in her seat to face Kip. "When she says 'just intel' "—she made air quotes with her fingers—"that's captain-speak for we're right back to hauling ass across the Via Casilina. Perfect. Just friggin' perfect."

"Well, I might as well pull the bandage off now," Rion said drily, knowing Lessa was going to love this part: "We're going to see Rouse."

Rion tried not to laugh at the murderous glare that blazed from Lessa's eyes, but sometimes Less was such an easy mark; swift to react, so full of young, passionate emotion. Having Lessa around was like having the little sister Rion had always wanted, complete with all the struggles that her childhood fantasies hadn't quite considered.

In the rearview mirror, she caught Kip's grinning reflection and smiled back.

Kip Silas was a decent guy with a calm, easygoing manner, and enough muscle to get the tougher jobs done. It also didn't hurt that he was a walking data chip of seemingly every class of ship in the known universe, and as engineers went, he was a damn fine one, a definite step up. All in all, she was happy with the new recruit so far.

The worst dive bar in New Tyne was tucked behind a one-story retail mall on the southern outskirts of the city. Despite the aging exterior, spotty electricity, and grungy interior, there were always vehicles in the lot and patrons at the bar.

"Looks . . . promising," Kip commented with a decided lack of enthusiasm as they left the truck.

When they approached the door, he paused at the sign nailed there—TINY BIRDS. "This is a joke, right?"

Unfortunately it wasn't. In fact, it was quite literal. The smell of stale rum didn't bother Rion so much as the distinct powdery musk that burned the insides of her nose and stuck in the back of her throat.

"Dear God," Kip uttered as he got his first look at the cages hung from the ceiling rafters, inside them hundreds of small birds the color of the sun and blue sky. Rouse's obsession had overtaken the building long ago, but no one here seemed to mind.

Tiny B's held the usual mix of patrons: a collection of humans, mostly at the bar; Kig-Yar who had taken up several tables along the far wall; and two Sangheili, in the far corner.

Rion headed for the table by the back-room door where Rouse conducted business. As she came into the light of the bar, recognition passed between her and one of the guys seated there.

Cottrell slipped off his bar stool, his eyes gleaming with drink and appreciation as they swept down Rion's body and back up again. "Baby. You're back."

For the hundredth time— "Not your baby, Cottrell."

A leer stretched his mouth. "Man, aren't you a sight for sore eyes. Damn, girl. Never seen fatigues look so fine. And to think I almost forgot what a hot piece of tail you—"

The gurgle that came from Cottrell's throat was intensely satisfying. Rion's grip on his scruffy neck tightened, the pressure making his bloodshot eyes bulge. Anger had ignited so fast that she'd reacted before her brain had a chance to catch up.

Should have walked on by.

Usually she did. But that particular phrase . . .

She squeezed harder. "Anything else you want to say to me, Cottrell?" He shook his head. "I think the next time I walk in here . . . I dunno . . . a 'Hey, Captain, how ya doing?' will work just fine."

"Sure, sure. Works fine," he rasped, clearly stunned by her reaction.

Cottrell was all bark and no bite. Rion knew that, but . . .

Reckless, volatile, lashing out . . . Rion had been accused of those things in the past, and rightly so. It had been a long time since she'd gotten this rattled, and it certainly wasn't her usual routine to play the badass. But Cottrell had said the wrong set of words, words that instantly revived memories of another bar, another time, into her mind quicker than a flashbang grenade.

Dinner with Dad.

Mom refused to take her, as usual. But Jillian stepped up and offered. Jillian was fun and gorgeous and always game for anything, and Rion adored her. Her five-year-old heart was beating so fast when they entered the lounge, so excited and nervous to see her father again . . .

But it wasn't her dad who met them—it was that horrible lieutenant, drunk, eyes gleaming as he leered at Jillian and made those foul comments. Rion wasn't sure what it all meant, but she knew it was bad. And when he turned his eyes on her and said she'd grow up to be a fine piece of tail . . . Jillian had lost it and struck the guy. Rion never knew fear like that before, when the lieutenant shoved her aunt against the wall, his forearm on her throat, pressing hard.

Too hard.

Then her father appeared like some avenging angel out of the ether. And—like her granddaddy was fond of saying—all hell broke loose.

"Cap," Lessa said sharply under her breath, poking Rion in the rib. "*Rion.*"

Rion blinked, realizing she'd moved on from the bar and was now standing in front of Rouse's table. And, of course, Rouse was watching her with his typical knowing, almost sagelike gaze. It was a look Rion knew well and one she found highly disconcerting.

Clearing her throat and giving the old man a tight smile, she slid into the booth as Rouse pulled his datapad over and made a few swipes before pushing it across the table. With a practiced eye, Rion examined the screen. "This the only image you have?"

He nodded. "It's clearly a ship. What kind"—Rouse shrugged and sat back with a twinkle in his eye—"remains to be seen. Your job to find out, salvager, not mine. My price is forty thousand credits for the location and twenty-five percent of sale."

Rouse tried, but he was a horrible negotiator. Rion's attention returned to the blurry image on the screen. It could have easily been mistaken for one of the many jagged gray rocks jutting up from the snow, but to a trained eye, the lines were unmistakable. "Ten thousand and ten percent."

Rouse held her gaze for a long moment, and Rion had to bite her tongue to keep from smiling. "Thirty and twenty," he said, obviously enjoying himself.

She slid the datapad back. "The wreck is old, probably picked clean two decades ago. And depending on the location, it could cost more to get there than it's worth, which means I need my credits. Offer stands at ten." She rubbed her cheek and took some time to think, time she didn't really need. "I would, however, be willing to cut you a deal on the sale end, though . . . say fifteen?"

"Ten thousand credits and fifteen percent." He thought it over for a minute, then nodded slowly. "I do see your point. The location is quite a hike. . . . all right, Captain, we have a deal."

Rion parked in the lot near the hangar bay where the *Ace of Spades* was docked, then hiked up a flight of stairs to catch the elevator to E-Level.

Ace was a *gorgeous* ship. Seven years in the making, she was a sleek Mariner-class transport ship refitted with so many bells and whistles that it made her one of a kind. Rion had no idea what the crew did with their own credits, but everything she made went back into the next job and from there into *Ace*. Her pride and joy had an advanced passive-sensor array, a military-grade slipspace drive, two pivoting fusion engines on each wing, six thrusters, a sensor-baffling suite, and already souped-up nav and comm systems that Niko had worked his tech magic upon. There wasn't much the ship needed anymore. Though, a smart AI would be nice. . . .

"You guys are never going to believe where we're going!" Lessa called as she jogged up the ramp and into the cargo hold.

Rion crossed the hold and headed for the steps. Cade was sitting one story up on the catwalk, performing maintenance on the track system. He stopped working as Rion looked up at him. "Meeting in the mess in fifteen," she told him. He gave her a curt nod and then returned to the job at hand.

That was Cade, all business. He was steady, reliable, and got the job done—the kind of man who didn't say much, but when he did, you tended to listen. A former marine, he brought order and efficiency to their small crew and was often the voice of reason when Rion wanted to run full tilt and push their operation to the limits.

Fifteen minutes later, the crew was seated around the mess table and Rion laid it all out for them. They might piss and moan about the lack of R&R, but in the end they were like her—no one could resist a score.

"The ship we're after is huge," Rion said. "I'm guessing old freighter, possibly military. We won't know until we get there, but if this thing hasn't been picked over yet . . ."

"Money in the bank," young Niko said with a cocky grin, linking his slim fingers behind his head and leaning back in his chair. "Can't beat that."

Kip glanced at him with a confused frown. "Unless it's military." He looked up at Rion. "Right? I mean, the UNSC's Salvage Directive states tha—"

"Yeah, we're all familiar," Lessa interrupted, rolling her eyes. "Report your find, claim your reward, and let their military salvage crew take over. Blah, blah, blah. The comical part is they think that way out here, we actually give a damn. Where was the UNSC when we needed them? They show up when it's convenient for *them* and expect us to tremble at the might of Earth's grand military." She snorted and eased back down in her seat. "Not happening."

"This is the Outer Colonies, Kip," Niko added. "You know as well as the rest of us that they can't and don't control everything. Hell, they have a hard enough time keeping control of what's left of the colonies these days. They should be glad we're out there recovering their goods."

Cade was leaning back in his chair, arms folded over his chest, observing the conversation in his usual stoic manner. He didn't have the same outward disgust as Lessa and Niko, but he had his own set of conflicts when it came to the military and the war. He'd been honorably discharged from the Marines, but his return to civilian life hadn't gone so well. There hadn't been a home or a family to return to, only glass. Kilometers and kilometers of glass . . .

Rion met his somber gaze. Once, they were like Lessa and Niko, but somewhere along the way, they'd moved beyond passionate debates on wars and politics and put their energy and loyalty into the only thing they could count on: themselves.

"The UNSC leaves most salvagers alone," Rion told Kip, taking control of the conversation. "We're not smugglers. We hunt tech, metals, and small arms, whether that be UNSC, Covenant, or civilian." She'd had this conversation with Kip when she hired him, but maybe she hadn't been completely clear in this regard. "We don't bring large arms and WMDs to market. Any military group is more than welcome to come to the clearinghouse and buy back their wreckage. I know for a fact the UNSC keeps a buyer shacked up in New Tyne just for that purpose. Probably cheaper for them to buy at auction than to pay the costs of their own salvagers and scouts. . . . The point is, we get our fee either way. And if we find that wreck is military and there's a datacore or nuke on board, you better believe I'll report it."

"It's a good job, Kip," Cade told him. "Stop worrying. Cap is fair and we make a decent living, better than most out here."

"I did my research on her," Kip replied. "Wouldn't be here otherwise." He shifted in his chair to study Rion, his lips twitching into a smile. "Good reputation. Eighty-five percent success rate. Best salvage ship out there . . . Not bad for a thirty-two-year-old military brat from Earth."

"Suck-up," Niko coughed into his hand.

She'd hardly considered herself a military brat, but Rion

didn't bother enlightening him. Instead, she shrugged it off. "You trying to butter me up, rookie? Because flattery gets you extra rations." She couldn't fault him for looking her up; she'd done the same to him, though more extensively than he'd ever know.

"So what's our destination?" Cade asked.

"Ectanus 45." Rion leaned over and pressed the small flat pad integrated into the center of the table's surface. A holographic star map appeared. Rion began zooming in on the star system until a large blue planet came into focus. "We'll bypass the planet. It's uninhabited, so we'll have no worries there. . . ." She turned the view slightly and stopped on the planet's moon. "This is our target. Eiro. It's tidally locked to the planet, but there's a narrow twilight ring that supports a small settlement. Our target is approximately fifty-six kilometers away from the twilight ring on the dark side of the moon. Location couldn't be better—too cold for habitation, but close enough to the ring that our winter gear should suffice. According to Rouse, the settlement has one communications satellite, two transport ships, and very little defense capability. As far as entering their airspace, we're good. They won't know we're there, and we'll have plenty of time to do our jobs."

"That's on the edge of the Inner Colonies, a border system. A long way off our usual route . . ." Cade said thoughtfully, leaning forward in his chair, completely focused on the map. "You sure about this?"

When he lifted his head, Rion met with a pair of grim eyes, those of a man who had seen war and knew more than anyone the price of taking risks, of jumping systems and hunting salvage that others would fight and kill for. "Yeah, I'm sure. It'll take a while, but it'll be worth it."

After a hard workout and an even harder sparring round with Cade, Rion hit the shower and then dressed in casual gear before returning to her quarters with a towel slung around her shoulders. Her muscles were weak and shaky. She'd pushed herself hard. Working out her demons. The usual.

Sitting down at her small desk, she stared off into nothing for a moment.

The demons were still there. Stronger than ever.

They'd left Venezian airspace and jumped an hour ago. And for the first time since seeing the grainy image on Rouse's datapad, she allowed herself to consider yet again the possibility.

She ran her hands down her face and let out a weary sigh. How long was she going to keep doing this to herself? How long would she let the past haunt her?

Forever, it felt like.

She'd been searching for ghosts since she was six years old, since her grandfather had sat her down and told her that her father had been lost. That's all. Just . . . *lost*. What did that mean exactly? What the *hell* did that mean? To a child those words had been utterly confounding. How many millions of families across the galaxy had been torn apart like hers? Fathers, mothers, sons, daughters. So many consumed by war, so many MIA and KIA, the list was unimaginable.

How did you bury a man who was lost? How did you grieve? Or move on?

Voices of her family, of her pediatrician and psychologist, echoed in her mind, putting terms and labels on her pain like Childhood Traumatic Grief. PTSD. Anxiety.

How had she grieved?

She'd built an entire life and profession on the foundation of loss.

Salvager.

Rion shook her head and gave a tired laugh.

Salvager. Her whole life spent searching, pushing ever onward, jumping from system to system, planet to planet, one wreck after another. Looking for a ghost ship. Somewhere along the way it had become routine, the drive to find answers eventually muted by days, years, decades, until her job was simply a job, a way of life. . . .

It had been a while since she'd thought about him.

She pulled open her desk drawer and retrieved her favorite holostill, setting the flat chip on the table and turning it on.

And there he was.

That cocky grin on his face always made her smile. Even now that she was a grown woman, he seemed larger than life. He'd been her hero, her protector, a rugged, capable kind of man, and a marine through and through.

With a heavy breath, Rion placed the image back in her desk. The data chip was there too, containing all of the messages he'd sent home for her. Sometimes, when she really wanted to torture herself, she'd listen to them.

But she'd had enough for one day.

TWO

The *Ace of Spades* settled into geosynchronous orbit above the dark side of Eiro. The twilight ring was just visible, a gray-blue haze outlining the moon's circumference.

"Have you located our target, Less?"

"That's a big ole affirmative, Captain. I have temp readings too. You guys ready for this?"

Niko swiveled in his comm chair, his knees bent, and his feet tucked under his bottom. "You mean ready to have my balls frozen off? Um. No. Not really."

Cade grunted in agreement. "Hear, hear."

"Fifty below zero."

"Woo. Hoo," Niko responded as dully as he could.

"It's a balmy seventy-five and blustery in the ring," Lessa added, ignoring Niko.

"Less and I will set her down," Rion told them. "The rest of you head to the locker room and suit up."

Lessa swiveled in her chair to face Niko as he got up. "Don't forget your earmuffs, little brother." She laughed as he shot a rude gesture behind his back. When he was gone, she returned to the job at hand. "Winds are looking bad down there."

From her position at main, Rion monitored their progress as *Ace* broke atmo, keeping an eye on Lessa as the young woman navigated the ship. Lessa was learning and improving with every mission, and soon Rion would be able to rely on her more often. "Adjust thrusters and keep us on target the best you can."

The closer they came to the surface, the more *Ace* was pushed around.

A kilometer out, things calmed down and the ship settled, but they'd been moved off target by two klicks.

"Sorry, boss."

"Winds were rough. You did fine. Correct your course and get us back on track."

Lessa plugged in coordinates and then rose slightly in her seat to get a better look at the landscape and the wreckage below. "It's pretty, isn't it, the snow? The wreckage sure blends in."

As they descended, Rion got a nice view of the bow, which jutted out of the snow at a thirty-five-degree angle. Small pockets of ice and snow had built up all over the hull, stuck in the angles and lines of the ship's design.

Ace's reverse thrusters engaged and they eased down next to the solemn metal giant, its hull filling the viewport as they descended. An icy shiver ran down Rion's spine as the telltale emblem of wingtips appeared, rising up from the clinging ice and snow. There was no mistaking even a portion of that symbol. United Nations Space Command.

Not his ship.

The lines are all wrong. . . .

Lessa had gone silent. The chatter from the guys down in the locker room had stopped; no doubt Niko had turned on the bulletin board so they could see the feed.

War had touched all their lives. They'd all experienced loss. They all had scars. . . .

Looking back, Rion realized how strange and surreal war could be to a child. Confusing. Chaotic. Frustrating. And her family had always tried to make life appear as normal as possible, pretending everything was going to be "all right."

Her young mind had known it wasn't all right. Her father being lost wasn't all right. Entire colonies being glassed wasn't all right.

Rion's anger and conflict had begun at such an early age. Hating the military because they refused to share information about her father, yet feeling pride in her father and all the soldiers out there fighting, in the absolute dogged determination of her race to survive.

Looking at this wreckage now made Rion realize she hadn't really reconciled anything from her past. Like carrion creatures, they were about to pick clean this beautiful old warship. There was some guilt in that. And yet this was all she had—the war was over and people had to make a living. But sometimes, some days, she wasn't sure of right from wrong anymore.

Her chest felt tight. *Another dark smudge, another karmic tally mark.*

"Sixty seconds," Lessa quietly said.

Rion moved her hands in a familiar pattern over her control panel. "Landing gear engaged."

"Captain?"

It was Cade's deep voice.

As Lessa went through shutdown procedures, Rion transferred control of *Ace* to her wrist comm. "Yeah, Cade," she answered, getting up and following Lessa from the bridge.

"How do you want to play this?" He cleared his throat. "If there are casualties."

Lessa stopped on the stairs, hands on the railing, and glanced over her shoulder. Rion was struck by how young Lessa seemed in that moment. She didn't look twenty-two, but more like a little girl, one who'd seen her fair share of casualties.

Despite the fact that they were salvagers, they rarely found remains. On the few occasions they had, it wasn't on a mass scale. There was no procedure or protocol for it. And yet, she was the captain. Her crew would look to her to do the right thing.

"We'll take a look around, see what we've got, and go from there."

She might be a carrion bird, but she wasn't heartless. And she sure as hell wasn't keen on working a burial ground.

The staging bay, which had been dubbed the "locker room" a long time ago, was equipped with an impressive array of gear for virtually any type of known weather and terrain. Rion walked past the crew, found her locker, and pulled out her gear.

Once she was ready, she grabbed her helmet and slid it over her head, then called for comm check. Three checks replied when there should have been four. "Kip, you good?"

"One sec," Cade said, grabbing Kip's forearm and lifting his wrist commpad, hitting a set of commands that showed Kip how to link communications and his HUD together with the rest of the crew. "Visual?"

"Yep, got it. Thanks, Cade."

Cade nodded, then smacked Niko's helmet as the kid walked by. "Don't forget your plasma cutters this time, yeah?"

Lessa led Kip to the carts, showing him how to release the cart and activate its grav plates. Once everyone was equipped with a cart and their tool bags, they were good to go.

The air lock disengaged and the hangar door came down slowly, the cold sweeping inside and bringing with it a swirl of snow. "All right, kids," Cade said. "Time to pick and strip."

"Hey, Cade? This bring back memories?"

If Rion was close enough, she would have hit Niko hard for such a dumb question. Lessa, however, was close enough to do it for her.

"Ow. What was that for? He *was* a marine, you know," Niko said under his breath. "Just asking."

"Yeah," Cade's calm voice came over the comms. "It brings back memories, kid."

"You're a moron, Nik," Lessa muttered.

Once they were outside, standing in front of the wreckage, the sheer size of the ship stunned them all into silence. The impact of it took Rion's breath away—she'd never seen anything like it.

"I know what this is," Kip said with awe. "It's a Halcyon-class cruiser." All heads turned to him.

"You're sure?" Rion was already scanning the hull with her commpad and waiting for verification.

"You don't need to scan it," Kip answered. "I had models of this thing when I was a kid. Wow. Never thought I'd see one in the flesh."

"Niko, run a radiation check. If there are still nukes on this thing, I want to know immediately."

"Roger that, Cap."

"At least we don't have to worry about the engines," Kip said, turning to the section of ship rising from ground level. "They're gone."

"I'm not getting any readings," Niko told them. "Probably used them up in whatever battle this old girl saw."

"We'll enter from the break over there," Rion said, moving forward.

As they came around the hull, a massive gaping mouth rose stories above them. "That's not a break. This thing's been cut in half," Niko said.

"A ship this size . . ." Kip started. "I'd say what's left here is a quarter of it, maybe."

"Look at the plating," Lessa said. "It's not jagged at all."

"Plasma damage," Cade told her. "Stuff can boil metal. Looks like she got beamed in two."

"Everyone pull up schematics. And watch your step. Kip and I will head for the bridge and see what's left of comms, nav, and weapons systems. Cade, you head for the armory—looks like there were several on this class of ship. Should be one or two near the bridge. Lessa and Niko, you take the med bay and cryo."

Decades of snow had built up, filling in the gouge the ship had left in the ground and covering what was probably several collapsed decks. It looked to Rion like they were entering the mouth of a giant cave.

It took Rion and Kip forty-five minutes to get to the bridge, having to backtrack several times until they found a passable route, which Rion had marked with sensors. So far, no casualties discovered.

"They could have abandoned ship in time," Kip said, echoing her own thoughts.

She'd have to report it. Whether there were casualties or not, the families of the crew deserved to know what happened.

"Blast doors are down," Kip said as they approached the bridge. "Look. The ship is the *Roman Blue*, Captain." The designation and ship's emblem were imprinted above the control panel near the door.

"You read that, Niko? R-o-m-a-n, space, b-l-u-e," Rion said.

"Searching now," he replied.

Kip turned to her. "What now?"

"Any luck on the armory, Cade?"

"One sec . . . Yep. Looks like a decent payload." His breath huffed over the comm as he moved around. After a few metallic bangs, he reported: "Thermite paste . . . body armor . . . jet packs. Some small arms, rifles. And heavy ordnance."

"Leave the heavies for the military and pack up the rest. Less, how's it looking your way?"

"Not bad, Cap. Med bay's got some nice SFGs, biofoam, the usual. Lots of damage though. Gonna see if the pharmacy is intact. Might be some salvageables there, depending on how some of this stuff fares in cold weather."

"Niko?"

"Cryo's in bad shape. Place is huge. A few pods we can take—looks like some were ejected . . . Control panels look good. I'll see what else I can find. And, Cap, there's nothing on chatter about the *Roman Blue*. She's a ghost ship."

"Kip, head to Niko's location and give him a hand with those pods."

Kip hesitated for a moment, the light emanating from his HUD illuminating his features. "You gonna report it?"

The way he was looking at her made her uncomfortable, like he was judging her, like he was some self-appointed moral compass. "Yeah, rookie, I'm going to report it."

He dipped his head, then made his way down the corridor. Rion watched him go. Yes, she'd report it. But she had a feeling the UNSC would never tell the families a damn thing. They'd

let sleeping dogs lie, whatever line they'd fed loved ones originally—KIA, MIA—would probably still stand. Why open old
wounds?

Because there were people like her who'd spent their entire
lives unable to move on, always wondering, always searching . . .

Standing on this ship . . . she could just as well have been
standing on her father's vessel.

Gripped with the need to know more, Rion told the crew,
"I'm headed to the captain's quarters."

She wanted information, if only for everyone else who'd been
denied it. The war was over. There was no reason to hide the resting place of the *Roman Blue*. After she reported it and the UNSC
took control of the site, Rion would give them enough time to
collect their goods and then she'd release the intel.

She had to crawl through bent metal to get inside the quarters.

Typical space—living and dining area, private bath, and two
bedrooms. Debris littered the floor, like a giant hand had lifted
the compartments, shook them, and set everything back down
again. Her boots crunched metal and glass. The wind howled
through an opening beyond one of the compartment walls.

A picture frame caught her eye. As she picked it up, glass bits
fell onto the floor. Two young boys stared back at her, their arms
around each other.

Rion set the picture down and made for the overturned table.
Some of its wires were torn, but the comm cables were still attached, disappearing through the floor. She righted the heavy
table and examined the large integrated screen on its surface.
The screen was busted, but she set to work dismantling the panel
and then searched inside the casing for a data chip.

There you are.

She took the chip and placed it in her commpad. A list of dates began pouring down the screen. Personal log dates of Captain William S. Webb, the first being March 10, 2531.

"*Holy shit.*" Rion's knees went weak. She grabbed the table for support.

Early 2531 was the last time she'd heard from her dad.

Voices immediately came over the comm, asking if she was all right.

"What? Yeah, fine. I'm fine. Just . . . stubbed my toe." She said the first idiotic thing that came to mind.

As the chatter died down, Rion pressed the date on the comm. She'd never get another chance like this to get inside the UNSC.

Crumbs, she was looking for crumbs.

CAPTAIN'S LOG: MARCH 10, 2531

A slim gentleman appeared on the screen, with gaunt eyes and lines across his forehead. His hair was light and speckled with gray. There was a fatalistic look in his expression, a weariness about him that evoked a deep sadness. He went through the formalities of stating his name and rank and ran through the day's events.

"*. . . a month of repairs before we can return to the fleet. Captain Hood has been reassigned to the frigate* Burlington *in a fleet-support role for the time being as I take command of the ship. I'm sure he'll make his way back to the front lines soon. God knows we need all the talent we can get. The admiral insisted I stay and witness the dressing-down he gave to the captain. It was . . . harsh, but deserved.*" The captain shook his head, obviously troubled a great deal by the event. "*Disobeying orders and engaging the* Radiant Perception *near Arcadia was reckless and foolish. He had no chance of defeating that destroyer. If Hood had picked up that log* *buoy and returned as ordered . . ."* The captain's shoulders sank a little. *"That buoy is out there somewhere, lost, picked up by the destroyer. . . ."* He sighed deeply, the weight of the war resting heavily on his shoulders. *"Godspeed to the folks on the* Spirit of Fire. *May they find their way home."*

Shock flared inside Rion, sending her stumbling back. She ended up sitting amid the debris, disoriented, her breath stalled in her lungs.

Her eyes began to sting. She gasped, remembering to breathe. Her pulse was wild, heart thundering so loud it filled her eardrums.

Somewhere in the din, she heard voices. The crew, no doubt, hearing the commotion. Unsure of what to do, she scrambled to her feet as a wave of pure adrenaline hit her.

Rion closed her eyes and willed herself to calm down as the ship suddenly shuddered hard, sending her flying forward, straight into the table. Pain shot through her hip as a loud, metal-lic groan echoed through the *Roman Blue.*

Quickly, she grabbed the data chip from her wrist and shoved it into her pocket. It was the most valuable thing she'd ever found in all her years of searching, and she'd be damned if she'd lose it now.

"What the hell was that?" she yelled over the comm.

The crew's responses came quick and jumbled.

Cade shouted above them all. "That's ordnance—someone's firing on the ship!"

Another round slammed into the *Roman Blue,* and the entire floor where Rion stood vibrated, then dropped a few centimeters. Damn it, it was going to give.

She took off at a dead run for the mangled door, diving through the small hole she'd crawled through just as the floor in the captain's quarters collapsed. Her momentum sent her rolling across the corridor, where she banged against the wall.

Her temper ignited as she got up. "I swear, if they hit my ship, I'm going to kill someone! Head out, people. *Now!*"

As Rion rushed down the wrecked corridor, a knot formed in the pit of her stomach because she knew she was the weak link, the farthest away from *Ace*. The crew was close together and would make it back at least fifteen to twenty minutes before she could, and that was a lifetime right now. "Get to *Ace*, go dark, and get her airborne as soon as you're all on board."

"Not without you." Cade's voice came over the comm with a ring of finality. "Not a chance in hell."

"Appreciate the love and all"—she dodged a metal plate as it fell from the ceiling—"but if they hit her, we've lost everything." She righted herself and started running again. "I can fend for myself. Lie low. You know I can. We've done this before, Cade, more times than I can count. I'll send a signal when I'm clear."

Several negatives filled her comm until Rion shouted at them to knock it off, get their heads on straight, do their goddamn jobs, and save her ship.

The comms finally went silent and all Rion could hear were the sounds of heavy breathing and pings of metal and shuffling.

"Damn it, Forge," Cade's voice broke the quiet. Rion smiled. He only used her last name when he was pissed. "I'll be waiting for your signal."

"Counting on it."

Purpose shot through her like lightning.

She wasn't dying today. Not now. Not when she'd found a crumb.

No, not a crumb, she thought as laughter bubbled up from some crazy part of her. She'd found a lead to a goddamn *ship.*

Spirit of Fire . . . *I'm coming for you.*

Dad . . . I'm coming for you.

PART TWO

LUCK BE A LADY

THREE

The *Roman Blue* shuddered again. Temperature warnings flashed across Rion's HUD as a superheated shock wave rolled through the vessel. The sizzle of burning metal hissed through her audio. Whoever was firing on the wrecked UNSC cruiser had gone from ordnance to plasma.

Not something she saw every day.

Over the years, she'd imagined the many ways she might meet her end, but *melting* had never been on the list.

In a matter of minutes, her cold suit had gone from asset to potential death trap; the thing wasn't designed to handle high exterior temperatures; it was meant to keep heat *in*. And if she didn't clear the *Roman Blue* soon, she could add roasting alive to her growing list . . . if the next blast didn't do her in first.

Metal blistered and groaned, eerie notes ringing through the passageways as walls and floors turned molten and supports gave way, entire sections crashing through levels. The walkway beneath Rion's feet began to dip starboard.

Her pulse beat wildly as she ran, dodging and ducking through an ever-changing maze of twisted and jagged alloy.

One more corridor to go.

She slipped around a corner and grabbed at a damaged railing. It broke from the bulkhead, sending her sliding backward and plowing into the opposite wall. Her neck snapped back and a crack echoed in her ears. A quick glance at the HUD showed a small fracture in the exterior shell of her helmet, but the damage was confined to the outer layer, one of many layers made of titanium nanocomposite fibers and plating. And those, thank God, were still intact.

As the remains of the *Roman Blue* continued its dip starboard, Rion drew on all her reserves and sprinted, as fast as the cold suit would allow, for the broken stairwell, counting each step in her head, knowing it'd take some time for the plasma cannon overhead to gear up for another blast.

Instead of taking the stairs one tread at a time, she leapt the distance and hit the landing with a *thud*. The weakened stairwell shuddered, slowly dropping away behind her as she bolted for the shafts of welcome daylight piercing through the wreckage.

The white glare from the moon's wintry surface was blinding, but not so much that she couldn't see what lay ahead. A few meters more and the deck simply disappeared into open space. She didn't slow down. Out was out, no matter how far she'd fall.

And if she was going to meet the ground, it would be as far away from the *Roman Blue* as possible.

At the edge of the deck, Rion shoved off with everything she had and sailed into the air.

On the bright side, the drop was only one story.

On the not-so-bright side, controlling her descent in the heavy suit was impossible. The earth and snow rose up to meet her with a vicious slap that stole her breath and sent her forehead slamming into her display. Her vision went black. Alarms rang in her ears and the taste of blood from a bitten lip trickled into her mouth.

With a groan, she rolled onto her back and blinked tightly several times until her vision cleared, only to find the HUD blitzing in and out. All around her, clouds drifted upward.

No, not clouds. It was steam. From her suit. A pained laugh bubbled in her throat. She'd come very close to catching fire after all.

The force of the ordnance explosions and plasma beam had pushed burning debris and snowmelt skyward, creating a strange fall of sleet and metal rain. Tiny fragments and ice tapped against her helmet, the sound mingling with the hiss of snow as bigger fragments met the frigid surface. With a wince, Rion sat up and brushed a few embers off her suit.

Just as the HUD corrected itself, a faint lavender glow began building in the clouds. Spurred by the telltale sign of heating plasma, Rion ignored the aches and pains, scrambled to her feet, and took off through the freezing slush and mud, pumping her arms and not looking back.

Her focus was on a large outcropping of rocks about two hundred meters away. But the longer she ran, the farther away they seemed. *Please don't glass the moon, please don't glass the moon.* A thread of panic started to unwind and she felt thrust back to a time when glassed planets were a horrifying reality. She had no idea who was attacking the *Roman Blue* or what capabilities they had, but she was praying like hell that the plasma beam was directed at a single target and not the entire moon.

Part of her wanted to break silence and call in *Ace* for immediate retrieval, but that was the anxious Rion talking, the scared Rion. The sane part of her knew the plasma beam would've been a hell of a lot more intense and encompassing if the intention was to glass Eiro. It wouldn't make sense to use a concentrated beam on the *Roman Blue* and *then* proceed with complete lunar destruction.

Her lungs and throat were on fire, and her thighs and calves screamed as she trudged on, unable to go any faster than a quick, uneven jog. Finally, she slid around the cover of the rocks, crawled up under the outcropping, and tucked herself into a crevice. Unlike being inside the *Roman Blue*, there was no Titanium-A plating to take the brunt of the blast, no walls and levels and metal to absorb and mitigate some of the potential heat.

Rion surveyed the vast snowy landscape through a narrow frame of rock, holding on to the hope that it wasn't the last view she ever saw.

The world flashed violet, then white.

Then the heat wave came, rolling over the landscape with a deep *whoosh*.

The interior of her suit became sweltering. The temperature surge and the HUD's flashing alarms brought on a roll of nausea that had her shutting down visual and audio before closing her eyes and hoping for the best.

When Rion opened her eyes, her view was gone, replaced by long, flash-frozen icicles barring the way out. She scooted away from the crevice and kicked at the icicles' thinner bottoms, breaking them enough to tummy-crawl out of her hiding spot. The ground had become ice, but she held on to the rocks, using them to pull herself to her feet and inch her way around the outcropping to get a good look at the *Roman Blue*.

Or rather, what was left of it.

The former UNSC cruiser was nothing but a smoldering mess, large chunks of debris sticking up like metal bones through a glowing, molten soup.

The clouds above the wreckage had faded once more to a dull, solemn gray.

Shaky and spent, she sat against the rock and let out a heavy sigh. Eiro hadn't been the target. And neither had she. Or *Ace of Spades*, for that matter.

She brought her hands up to rub her face, but when gloves hit helmet, she let out a sharp laugh. The lines of sweat rolling down her skin created a near maniacal need to rip off her suit and wipe those feathery, itchy lines away.

But as much as she wanted to, she had no desire to be flash-frozen like the land around her. So she glanced skyward again. Whatever ship had been there before was probably long gone. There was nothing to salvage, no reason to send a landing party. The damage was done.

Cowards.

No respectable salvager would destroy a perfectly good and profitable wreck. Salvagers had a code—a shaky, unspoken one, but a code nonetheless. An honor system most of them lived and worked by.

Firing on someone else's claim, obliterating it, putting lives in danger, even killing to get the best scraps . . . that might have been how things were done during the Covenant War and its immediate aftermath. But that was then, a time when the entire galaxy was in a constant state of flux, when planets and colonies were emerging from the wreckage and rebuilding, when governments began taking shape once again, when chaos and power grabs were a common enough occurrence.

During the war and in the early postwar days, salvagers were a crazy bunch—Rion included. It had been a free-for-all, ruled by the fastest and most heavily armed. But over the years, and after a few sobering displays of violence, most salvagers had come to their senses and begun working with more civility. There was plenty of scrap to go around. The war had seen to that.

There were only a few groups she could think of that would want the *Roman Blue* and all it contained gone, to remain a ghost ship forever.

Its makers, for one. The UNSC.

ONI, for another.

Nothing else made much sense.

The chance that this was about some other salvager's attempt at personal revenge was slim. Rion had made her share of enemies, had beaten rivals to scrap enough times that more than a few of her competitors held deep grudges. But a true salvager wouldn't destroy the goods in the process.

Leaning forward, elbows resting on her knees, she checked her commpad. Fifty-two minutes of oxygen left. The wreckage had begun to cool, parts of it already becoming glass, black jagged smears on the snowy surface of the moon.

Finding that link to her father and then having anything else she might have found immediately ripped away . . .

Talk about being sucker punched.

And as much as she wanted to move forward and make tracks, it was too soon to break silence. While chances were small that the attacking ship was still around, she wouldn't run the risk quite yet. *Ace* would never stand against an enemy that could do the damage she'd just witnessed. And if Rion lost the *Ace of Spades*, she might as well throw in the towel and sell chatter boxes from a kiosk in a mall somewhere on Earth.

Ace of Spades was more than a ship. It was her workhorse, her home, her sanctuary. Above all, it was her escape, her means to leave whenever she wanted to leave, to fly, to hunt, to explore. . . . The universe was hers to navigate because of that ship, and she'd be damned if she'd ever let anything change that.

So she sat. And she waited.

FOUR

As the *Ace of Spades* descended to Rion's location, she pushed to her feet with ten minutes of oxygen to spare. Watching her ship always made her pause. While Mariner-class vessels were designed to operate with a small crew and carry a large payload, they were also things of beauty—fierce, fast, menacing, and sleek. And with the black ablative coating on the hull, her ship had taken on an even darker edge.

The coating was an expensive splurge and required regular maintenance, though it was rare that *Ace*, unlike military vessels, was fired upon or scratched enough to require consistent refinishing. The small number of private firms now producing civilian-grade stealth technology charged an arm and a leg. But if there was money in the bank, Rion usually sprang for any tech that would give them an edge. And in this case, the price was worth every credit because it allowed *Ace* to engage in more . . . *delicate* salvage ops. . . .

Ace's thrusters should have stirred up a small blizzard around her, but everything was frozen solid from the plasma melt and refreeze. She'd already spoken briefly over comms, but other than a quick update with the crew, she'd remained silent, not ready to chat or delve into details. As irritating as her suit and itchy skin had become, she had needed the time on Eiro to gather her thoughts and let events sink in.

One small chip, and everything was about to change.

As the ramp descended, there was no mistaking the man waiting to disembark, despite the cold suit and helmet he wore. While Rion could only see her reflection in Cade's visor as she approached, she knew that behind the tempered glass composite there was probably a very pissed off ex-marine, one who was hardwired to never leave a crewmember behind.

Cade paused in front of her, taking in her charred suit and damaged helmet. His deep voice broke through the low hum of audio static. "Suit looks like shit, Forge." Then he turned and headed back up the ramp.

Yep. He was pissed.

On more than one occasion, the two had nearly come to blows about her tactics. But ultimately, in the end, it was her ship. And when it came to making sure *Ace* was safe, there was no one she'd ever ask to stay behind but herself.

"We're in," Rion said, removing the straps to her gloves with quick, jerky movements as the ramp came up. The air lock engaged. She ripped the gloves off and let them drop to the floor. "Get us out of here." Her helmet joined the discarded gloves.

As Cade continued to the locker room to de-suit, Rion ran her hands and nails all over her itchy face. Instant gratification shot beneath her skin, the relief utterly satisfying. Once that little ritual was over, she picked up the gloves and damaged helmet, then headed after Cade.

After tossing the helmet into her locker, she unzipped the cold suit, exposing her damp, sweaty torso to the cool air. She was bruised too, her muscles already growing stiff. Sitting down, she went for her boots, but the damn strap on the left one had completely melted.

"We headed back to Venezia?" Lessa asked over the ship-wide intercom.

"No." Rion struggled with the strap. "Niko, I want you to find the nearest comm sat. We're going to patch in, boost our search capabilities, and do some digging. Are we clear on radar?"

"Not a ship in sight," he answered.

"Good. Plot a course, then."

Cold suit hanging off him, Cade pulled his knife from his belt, leaned over, and slipped the blade beneath the strap of her boot, slicing it clean. He remained eye level with her for a beat, and she was met with questioning brown eyes. "You good?" he asked.

"Fine."

He straightened, slid his knife back in his belt, and turned back to his locker, shrugging the rest of the way out of the suit.

Her boot finally came free and she had to bite down the urge to wing it across the room. Once she was down to her flight suit, she shoved her things into her locker. "I'm gonna hit the shower. I want everyone in the lounge in thirty minutes."

Under the spray of a lukewarm shower, Rion let her thoughts drift to earlier aboard the *Roman Blue*. Crawling into the captain's quarters, finding the chip, feeling that great surge of shock and renewed hope when the captain mentioned the *Spirit of Fire* . . . it had been electrifying.

But it was only a moment, a short blip in a lifetime of wondering and questioning and searching. There were more than two decades of time since that log entry. And now that reality had set in, it seemed impossible that answers might still be out there. The chip might simply be another painful reminder, a tiny crumb on a phantom trail that spanned the entire galaxy.

They're out there, Lucy, her grandfather had often said. It was a phrase repeated in her household a hundred times over.

She remembered the day those words had been spoken for the last time. From a hospice bed, her grandfather's thin hand tightly wound in hers, the skin cracked and dry like paper, but surprisingly still strong. *I know he's out there. My boy is out there. You find him and bring him home. Do what the rest of us couldn't.*

It was a terrible burden to put on a teenager's shoulders. But even then she'd understood his need. He hadn't meant to lay that task on her; he'd simply wanted assurance, some kind of closure, something to allow him to close his tired eyes, rest easy, and fade away.

And when he was gone, Rion was well and truly alone.

She'd never been close to her mother, and her Aunt Jillian had left Chicago a few years prior, taking a dream job at some corporate law firm in Sydney. And eventually, that city had become Jillian's tomb. . . .

After her grandfather's funeral, Rion had packed her bags and left.

Ran was more like it. Right to the recruitment center to enlist.

She'd walked by the center's front door three times in the span of half an hour, uncertain and never really getting the sense of rightness that she expected. She was a Forge, for God's sake. It *should* have felt right. Instead, she felt like a fraud. Hell, her father had enlisted when he was sixteen. No hesitation. Probably burst right through the front door and demanded to be signed up.

Yet Rion couldn't muster the nerve or the passion.

So she headed to the bar down the street, parked herself on a stool near the door, expecting to be kicked out once the bartender got a good look at her, and fought an inner battle with herself. Her reasons were all wrong. She wasn't enlisting because she wanted to do good or save the world or be a hero. So why was she? Why had she gone there?

To be close to her father and grandfather, no doubt. By doing what they had done, perhaps she wouldn't feel so utterly alone.

"You got ID on you?" the bartender asked.

Rion had glanced up at the hard face and sighed. "Yeah, but it'll only get me booted out the door." She slid off the stool and grabbed her pack.

"Ah, give the kid a break, Hal!" A group of four men and one woman occupied a booth in the corner by the door. They were a coarse-looking bunch, travel-weary and rough around the edges. "She looks like she could use a drink!"

Hal shrugged indifferently. "Rules are rules, Birger." He nodded to the door. "Beat it, kid."

"Never mind Hal. Come join us," the man named Birger called as she hiked her pack over her shoulder. To this day, Rion wasn't sure what made her stop. Maybe it was the look of them. Different. Out of place. Not only rough, but capable; their manner and their eyes held weight and worldliness, like they'd seen and done it all and had the scars inside and out to prove it.

Her feet had moved before her brain had caught up, and she found herself in front of their table.

"You look lost, girl," the woman said with a smile and a deep accent Rion couldn't place. She was older, forties, maybe, with gray hair in two fat braids, sharp ice-blue eyes, and a strong, striking face. "You running away, then?"

Rion gestured in the recruitment center's direction. "Enlisting."

Birger laughed. He too was graying—a big, burly giant of a man, his presence equal to his size. "Eh. Why enlist when you can sail the starry skies without all the killin' and dyin'? How old are you, child?" he asked, eyes narrowing.

"Eighteen," she lied.

"I was your age." He turned to the woman seated next to him. "Unn here was sixteen."

"When you enlisted?" Rion asked.

Birger smiled. "When we"—he pointed to the ceiling—"left Mother Earth. There's gold in the stars, if you know where to look."

"You're pirates," Rion blurted out before she could stop herself. They certainly had the look about them.

Birger threw his head back and howled with laughter, the sound echoing throughout the bar and probably out into the street. The others chuckled, though Unn simply smiled and said: "*Salvagers*, girl. *That's* where the gold's at."

"We're talkin' credits just floatin' out there for the takin'." Birger spoke with his hands and his entire body, proceeding to weave a fantastic tale that captured Rion's attention and her heart. *Here* was the passion she'd been looking for. Adventure . . . stars . . . planet after exotic planet . . . a life spent wandering and trading and bartering.

Thoughts of the recruitment center were immediately abandoned, and Rion never looked back.

Those first few years on Bjorn Birger's cargo ship, *Hakon,* were everything he claimed they would be. Of course, he'd left out the harsh, horrific things: dodging in and out of war zones posed the potential not only for riches, but for threats unlike anything Rion had imagined. When a situation developed in the middle of nowhere, you couldn't exactly run away. You had to push through, deal with whatever problem loomed. She learned firsthand, and many times, that when things went wrong, they went very, very *wrong.* Starvation, death, betrayal, torture, you name it. They might have called themselves salvagers, but they sure as hell had acted like pirates.

And as time passed, the older the Birgers became, the less control they had over the crew.

Their loss meant Rion's safety teetered on the edge. They stopped protecting her, whether they realized it or not, too old to care, too distracted to see, too disinterested—or, by Unn's way of thinking, *necessary* for Rion's development as a future leader.

In the end, Rion had taken matters into her own hands.

On her twenty-fourth birthday, she killed a man. In the cargo hold, blood on her face and hands as the entire crew looked on, placing bets and eager to shove the loser out the air lock. Her fight with Sorely had been brewing since the day he joined the *Hakon.* . . .

She'd earned a measure of respect that day, and a measure of distance. She'd slept better that night than she had in years.

None of it came easy.

She'd fought for every scrap, every ounce of respect. And when Birger began to decline, Unn had taken Rion into her confidence and together they began laying the groundwork to maintain control of the *Hakon.*

Keen-minded, sharp-tongued, and quick with knives, Unn

Birger could have captained the *Hakon* for years after Bjorn Birger's death, but once he was gone, so was her ambition. And so she bequeathed her knowledge and lifelong advice to Rion.

Unn had died a year after Birger. Natural causes, ironically.

By that time, Rion held complete control of the ship. She could barter and manipulate just like Bjorn, and pilot and wield a knife better than Unn. She surrounded herself with those she could trust, and if she had the slightest doubt, they'd be off at the next station. Or, if the offense was great enough, the air lock sufficed—and she'd only had to do that once for the rest of the crew to fall in line. . . .

Rion shrugged the old memories away as she stepped out of the shower, dried off, dressed, and then made for the lounge.

The *Ace of Spades* was a decent-size ship, but she wasn't huge on crew space. Most of her volume was reserved for cargo. There were five crew quarters, the captain's quarters, a mess/lounge combo with observation deck, a med bay with cryo for eight, and a small attached gym with showers. Everything else beneath them was storage space, support systems, and engineering.

Rion went right for the food dispenser to retrieve an energy bar and a vitamin-and-electrolyte-infused water. Lessa was lounging in one of the swivel chairs at the table, smiling at something Kip had said, while Niko stared at Kip with a frown, his brotherly suspicions finally kicking in. For as smart as he was, it had taken Niko a while to pick up on the vibes his older sister was throwing Kip's way.

Cade was standing at the observation deck, hands clasped behind his back as he stared out into the black void of space.

Rion approached the long table anchored in the middle of the room. "Where are we on the comm sat?" she asked Niko.

Reluctantly, he withdrew his gaze from Kip. "There's one in this system, around Chi Rho."

"You get any readings of that ship before going dark?"

"You mean before you had us abandon you?" he asked.

Okay, so make that two people pissed. Possibly four.

Rion arched an eyebrow, one that asked Niko if he really wanted to start this fight. He glared at her for three petulant seconds before backing down.

"Before we took off," he finally said, "we logged a few readings as our mystery ship broke stealth to fire. More like nonreadings. No real signature, energy levels read like a small tug. I mean, we could have picked up more, but you said to go dark, so . . ."

Rion released a tired breath. "How many times have we had to go dark to avoid military or rebels or fringe?" She waited for someone to answer, but no one did, her point made. Honestly, she was a little irritated by the general mood in the lounge. "*I* make the call. And if I can't, Cade does." She glanced at him as he walked to the table. "He'd do the same to protect you and the ship. Without *Ace*, we have no way home, no way off whatever planet we're on. This ship was *meters* from the *Roman Blue*. If you hadn't left when you did, she'd be gone right now, and we'd be freezing our asses off on Eiro *permanently*. Don't any of you ever think I won't make the hard calls. And if that means leaving me behind until it's safe, then that's what'll happen."

Every eye in the room went downcast. Except, of course, for Cade's. He shrugged. "Hard to go dark when your captain is in the middle of a plasma beam."

"I wasn't in the middle." But she did understand the point. Had it been one of the crew down there, she probably would have gone and done something monumentally reckless. But then again, it was her call to make.

"So now what?" Kip asked. "There's no way to track that ship."

"We're not going to track it."

Their confusion bordered on comical. Even Cade's usually stoic face contorted into a puzzled frown. Rion leaned her hip on the edge of the table and swallowed a bite of her energy bar. "Whoever commanded that ship had a job to do. And they did it. The *Roman Blue* is completely unsalvageable."

Lessa frowned. "And . . . aren't we mad about that?"

"Yeah, we're pissed," Rion admitted. "But think about it. With the kind of stealth Niko is talking about and the firepower they had . . . this wasn't about us. Who benefits by destroying the *Roman Blue*? Not salvagers, not smugglers . . . not any faction I know of."

"Military," Cade answered.

"But why would they do that?" Kip sat back in his chair, his expression skeptical. "The amount of heavy ordnance and small arms left on the ship . . . It doesn't make sense they'd just sacrifice it all."

"They would if they wanted the *Roman Blue* to stay lost," Rion said.

"You think they came upon us by chance?"

"No. I think we were tagged at some point. To keep an eye on what we'd find. They already keep tabs on Nor and some of the other surplus houses along the trade route. Makes sense they'd tag salvagers too." And worse yet, rumor had it that military wasn't the only operation guilty of tagging. Fringe groups, marauders, and fragments of whatever was left of the Covenant wanted in on salvager scores as well, letting the pros do all the work and then swooping in to take the payload.

Three crews had gone missing in the last year.

And Rion, along with the rest of the salvagers along the Via Casilina, was beginning to suspect there was a lot of truth to the rumors.

Niko grew pale. "There's no way we were tagged." But his look said he wasn't so sure. "Ah, shit." He pulled up one of the displays integrated into the table and starting running scans.

"Wait a minute," Lessa said, still baffled. "If we don't care about that ship, then why are we heading to a comm sat? What exactly are we looking for?"

And damn if that question didn't make Rion's nerves shoot right to the surface. She downed the last of her water in an effort to gain a few seconds of composure. Talking about her past was a rare occurrence, but as of now, it was about to be the driving force for everything to come.

"I'll make this as brief as I can. . . ." She drew in a steady breath and set the water down. "You were right before, Kip. For a very short time, I was a military brat. I come from a very long line of soldiers. My father was a sergeant in the Marines. When I was five, he was commissioned to a refitted Phoenix-class colony ship called the *Spirit of Fire*."

As she paused, Kip glanced up sharply. "I've heard of that ship. . . . I'm sorry."

Rion nodded her thanks. "Official story says she was lost with all hands. But a lot of us, the other families, never really believed it. We heard so many conflicting reports. The things my grandfather learned from his military contacts suggest the Missing-In-Action designation only changed to Lost-With-All-Hands because the brass decided we needed closure. What we needed was the truth. And for us, until we learn otherwise, the ship remains missing. My father and the other eleven-thousand-plus crew on board remain missing."

A heavy weight seemed to settle in the room, and time stretched. Rion's blood pressure had risen with every word, each one simple and concise, but weighted down by an immeasurable amount of history and hurt.

Lessa lifted her head, her gaze on Rion, fixed and speculative. "Why are you telling us this now?"

"Because I found something on the *Roman Blue*, something that might lead me to answers. And I can't turn my back on it. I can't go back to salvaging and jumping the trade routes until I sort this out." She reached into her pocket and set the chip on the table. Everyone leaned forward.

"What's that?" Kip asked.

"Answers."

Cade took the chip and inserted it into the table's holo-display. They all watched as the holographic list of journal dates appeared.

"Go to the last entry," Rion said quietly.

Cade selected it and they watched the same video journal that had shocked Rion back on Eiro. Captain Webb's tired appearance, the defeat in his voice, the utter weight of the war . . . As Rion watched it again, it left her feeling spent and hollow.

When it was over, no one spoke. Then Cade turned to her. "You want that buoy."

Goose bumps spread up her arms. *More than anything.* "Yeah. I'm going after the *Radiant Perception*. I'm going to find that buoy and I'm going to find out what happened to the *Spirit of Fire* and her crew."

"Is this the part where you say it's personal and you don't expect any of us to come along?" Niko asked with suspicion. "You'll drop us wherever we want to go, just say the word, blah, blah, blah—"

A smile tugged Rion's lips. "I don't expect any of you to come along. I don't know where this is heading or how long it'll take. And I don't plan on stopping until the trail runs cold."

Silence descended in the lounge as her words sank in.

"But you should also know," she continued, "a trip like this still has the potential to pay out big."

"*Radiant Perception* was a Covenant vessel," Cade said with a slow grin.

Rion returned the grin.

"Um, okay, what are we missing?" Niko glanced between them.

"Salvage gold," Cade replied. "Salvage gold."

FIVE

Ace of Spades, Ectanus 45 system, four hours from Chi Rho

"**K**ip, will you pull up a CPV-class heavy destroyer schematic?"

Once the image hovered above the table, Rion explained: "During the war, nearly every Covenant vessel carried on board something called a luminary. The device was specifically designed to pick up signals emitted from Forerunner technology. The Covenant was big on finding and using the Forerunners' advanced tech to—as we all know—wipe humanity from the galaxy. Luminaries were key pieces to aid their cause."

"How is it I've never heard of one?" Niko asked.

"From what I've gathered from my digging and from ex-Covenant willing to talk, the Covenant had a pretty rigid protocol. It was called the Writ of . . . Security, Sanctity, something like that. Either way, it was designed to protect their sacred objects from falling into what they considered 'unclean hands.' The writ ordered the destruction of the luminary aboard any vessel should that vessel be compromised. They'd rather destroy their own tech and ships than let us get ahold of Forerunner artifacts."

"So finding one means we'd have our very own Forerunner-artifact sniffer," Lessa said, clearly warming up to the idea and its potential.

Niko leaned back and linked his hands behind his head. "Salvage gold. I like it."

"And this *Radiant Perception*," Kip said. "If we do find it . . ."

Rion turned off the holo-image. "Chances are we won't. Destroyers are like luminaries. You don't come across them every day, and if you do, they're already in the hands of those who could wipe us off the map. But if that vessel is out there, or even part of it is sitting in some shipyard somewhere, it's possible we might find a luminary that wasn't destroyed. And I might find my buoy."

"It's a big galaxy," Cade said at length.

"It is," Kip agreed, slowly shaking his head, a thoughtful expression drawing his brows. When he looked up, Rion was surprised to see possibility in his gaze. "But I swear I never thought I'd see a battlecruiser either, so . . ."

The rest of the crew started smiling, then laughing, and Rion stood there rather shocked that no one had outright bailed on her or even presented the slightest hesitation.

She went to the cabinet and pulled out a precious bottle of Alt Burgundy. "I think this calls for a drink."

Cade retrieved glasses and they toasted to finding answers.

Before they took a sip, Niko added, "And here's to weeks stuck on the ship with my irritating sister. If it's too long, I'm going in cryo."

"To weeks successfully avoiding my idiot brother," she shot back. "And finally having time to finish my Mindirian blanket."

"You've been working on that thing for two years," Niko said, rolling his eyes. He lifted his glass. "Fine. To finishing the god-awful, hairy-ass beast of a blanket."

"It's wool! And I'm not going to sleep with it. It's going on the wall. It's decoration. Imbecile."

"What about you, Kip?" Rion asked.

He thought for a moment, then raised his glass. "Here's to exploring the universe and finding your father."

Amen. Now *that*, everyone could drink to.

"Here." Rion glanced over her shoulder at the sound of Cade's voice. He approached with another glass of Alt Burgundy. The crew had left the lounge some time ago, and Rion had gone to the observation window to think. Soon Chi Rho would appear and fill the view with something other than the blackness of space.

She took the offered glass. "Thanks."

Cade remained silent, lurking behind her. At five-ten, she wasn't short by any means, but when Cade came this close, she felt petite. Part of her wanted to lean back and settle against his frame, to steal some warmth, to feel some measure of comfort and stability, but she remained stiff. As warm as the alcohol was going down, it didn't alleviate her tension.

"That buoy is probably long gone," she said after a few moments.

"Or could be the UNSC already recovered it."

If that were the case, Rion hoped she never found out the truth, because if the UNSC had located that buoy and kept secret what happened to her father and the *Spirit of Fire*, she wouldn't be able to stop herself from doing something foolish.

"More than likely, they never recovered it," she said. "I mean, think about it. At the time, the Covenant was coming through, glassing planets. The military was scrambling, trying to figure out the threat . . . to survive and save anyone they could." It must have been a sobering, chaotic time for humanity and a huge weight on the shoulders of a military tasked with stopping an alien invasion right on the heels of insurrection within its own colonies. A lost buoy wouldn't have been on anyone's radar, not when it was a struggle just to stay alive.

That the buoy still existed at all would be a miracle.

But then, all manner of things were finding their way back into circulation. In postwar, anything was possible.

Cade moved to stand beside her. "If the *Radiant Perception* picked up the buoy, they would have deciphered it if they could. Might have gone after your father's ship. . . ."

In her early days on the *Hakon*, she'd followed in the wake of UNSC fleets, remained on the edges of one battle after another. She'd witnessed the real damage wrought when two warships came together. If the *Radiant Perception* had found the *Spirit of Fire*, the outcome wouldn't have been good. . . .

"A lot could've happened," Cade said when she didn't respond.

In the last twenty-six years, the possibilities were endless. Even though she'd finally found a mention of her father's ship, Rion was well aware that she was embarking on an impossible mission, an outrageous attempt to find a tiny grain of sand in a galaxy full of stars. . . .

She took another sip, welcoming the burn in her throat and the spread of fire through her belly. Some of her stress finally eased, allowing her to lean against Cade's shoulder. He responded by slipping an arm around her back. "When I learned my family was gone . . ." He paused, seeming unsure how to continue. A heavy sigh escaped him. "Yeah, if there was any doubt, any hint that one of them made it out alive . . . I'd never stop looking. Never."

More than anyone, Cade understood her drive. And yet she couldn't help the sharp twinge of guilt that came with his words. Because he had lost everyone—and she had not.

"What is it?" he asked.

She gave a slight shrug. "I still have family. I could be with my mother even now. I could stop all this and go back to Earth, if she's still there. . . ." But she'd opted to run, and to keep on running to the very edge of human-occupied space. "Instead I'm out here in the dark, chasing ghosts."

Cade's grip on her tightened, a soft squeeze to tell her that he was on her side. "You're not one to stay grounded, Forge. A stationary life, it's not for everyone. Out here . . . it calls to people like us. Calls so hard we walk away even from those we love."

She tossed an unimpressed look his way. "Is that supposed to make me feel better?" Because that little nugget of truth only solidified her guilt.

His soft chuckle warmed her as much as the last bit of burgundy she'd thrown back. "Hey. I tried. Was working for a while."

In the end, though, Cade was right. They'd answered the call, and they both had to live with their decisions. Rion knew if she had to do it all over again, she'd still walk away. She'd still answer the call to the stars. She was cut from the same cloth as every other Forge who came before her. Her grandfather had often said that Forges had wanderlust in their blood—that and a thirst for adventure. On bad days, when his mind broke, he'd change that last part to "a thirst for killin'."

She'd never had bloodlust, but the wanderlust? That was there in spades. Always on the move, always going, always being pulled . . . While she had very few memories of her dad she vividly recalled his restless energy. On leave, he'd be jumpy, like he couldn't quite figure out how to live a civilian life. When his time was up, he was sad to go, but even at her young age, Rion could tell a part of him was relieved to get his feet off the ground and back into the sky.

Her mother could tell it too. Their marriage had been strained since before Rion was born. Neither one could claim the title of perfect spouse; they both had their faults. But sometimes Rion wondered if her mother envied her own daughter—maybe even hated her a little—for all the time and attention John Forge gave to Rion when he was home.

"We all have our demons," Cade said, his voice dropping. "And our regrets."

She let her head rest on his shoulder. He pulled her close and Rion's thoughts settled.

She and Cade were alike in many ways. The similarities had led them first into friendship, then into bed, and eventually into tumultuous times. Their relationship cycled around those stages like a planet orbiting a star. But always, no matter what, theirs was a deep, abiding friendship. He was her constant, and she was his. And in the confines of a ship in deep space, the reality of having someone you could count on was immeasurable.

SIX

Ace of Spades, 400,000 kilometers off Chi Rho

Checking File Systems..... DONE...
Checking Security...... DONE...
>>>>>>>>>>>>>
ONI FIELD PAD
LOG IN: ********
PASSWORD: *************
>>>>>>>>>>>>>
Encryption Code: OCTWTF
Clearance Level: H
ACCESS GRANTED

To: Hahn
From: 67159-021127

Location: Ectanus 45
Found: Halcyon-class cruiser, *Roman Blue* on Eiro.
Destroyed by unknown vessel. **NOTE:** *Was that you?*
Recovered: Captain's personal log chip mentioning buoy
dropped by *Spirit of Fire*. Date of drop unknown. Date of
log: March 10, 2531. It's assumed the buoy was picked up
by Covenant destroyer *Radiant Perception* near the planet
Arcadia. **Current:** Proceeding to Chi Rho orbital comm sat
to research the whereabouts of the destroyer.
NOTE: *Captain Forge is hell-bent on retrieving the buoy.
Instructions?*

Agent 67159-021127 watched the cursor on the datapad blink for
approximately thirty-nine seconds.

Had it been ONI firing upon the *Roman Blue* today? If so,
why hadn't they waited for Rion to leave the wreckage? Had they
wanted her to die? No. That wasn't what they'd told him when
he was recruited. They wanted to use her; they'd made that very
clear. She was an asset, a successful Outer Colony salvager who'd
made such a name for herself that she warranted keeping an eye
on for what she might find.

And Rion Forge found a lot of things.

The screen lit up.

Transmission received.
Report next destination.
END

SEVEN

Lessa found Rion on the bridge, sitting at comms, already researching the *Radiant Perception*.

She'd been surprised to learn about the captain's past. Usually, Rion kept a tight lid on her personal life, and for a people person like Lessa, it made her wildly curious. She wanted to know more about the woman who had rescued her and Niko from what would've been a very short life on Aleria.

When Rion had caught her and Niko in the bazaar on Aleria and discovered the truth of what they'd been trying to do, Lessa had been relieved. She was tired of ripping people off, tired of the goddamn heat and never-ending drought, tired of grit always in her eyes and mouth, of avoiding the courier guilds and having to pay a portion of whatever they stole to whatever guild happened to gain control from one month to the next. It was exhausting.

And Niko had been changing, becoming more and more like them with every passing day. More reckless, desensitized to violence . . . She was scared to death of losing him and scared of being alone.

It had been a gamble from the start, targeting Rion. The tall, dark-haired captain moved through the bazaar with a confident presence, sharp eyes scanning the stalls, expression alert and ready, yet relaxed too, like she'd be just as comfortable shopping the bazaar as she would taking on a direct assault.

Lessa envied her.

At first she'd just watched and followed. Owing to the heat, Rion had worn fatigues paired with a black tank top and a pistol strapped to her thigh. The sides of her dark hair had been braided back and tied into a bun. Smart. Lessa knew from experience that having your hair fisted and used as leverage in a fight was never a good thing.

Trying to rob Rion Forge had turned out to be the best day of her life.

And Rion didn't even know.

Well, that wasn't entirely true. She could tell the captain had gotten the gist of things real quick—what their life must be like and how it most likely would end up had they stayed on Aleria. With a median life span of forty-five years, Aleria wasn't exactly a hotbed of promise and hope.

More like a hot mess of fear and despair.

The way Lessa saw it, she owed Rion. So if the captain wanted to search the entire galaxy for her father, then Lessa was game.

"I'm sorry about your father," she said, startling Rion from her research. Lessa bit her lip and stared down at a fingernail, picking at it nervously. As much as she loved the crew, none of them were very big on talking, but sometimes a girl just needed to chat. . . . "I don't really remember my parents."

Rion turned her full attention to Lessa. "Did they pass away?"

"What?"

"Your parents. Did they pass away?"

"Oh. Um. I don't know. Probably. There's a lot of young parents on Aleria. They go into the mines and never come out. Or they come out sick. Or they go off smuggling. . . . Do you remember him, your dad?"

"I was young, but the memories I do have . . . Yeah, they're crystal clear."

"Do you look alike?" As a child, Lessa would always look at faces. In the bazaar, in the mines, in the tent cities, always looking for a resemblance to Niko or herself, always wondering who they belonged to. . . .

"My grandfather used to say I was the spitting image of my dad, only 'a hell of a lot prettier.' When my dad would come home on leave, my grandfather would tease him about it." A grin lingered on her lips as she remembered. "My dad would smile and say the ladies found him pretty enough."

"They seem like fun people."

"Fun and loud and argumentative. It was always a whirlwind when my dad came home. A quick whirlwind, and then it went back to being . . . quiet."

"What about your mom?"

"Still on Earth, I guess. We were never close." By the way Rion's face fell, Lessa could tell it was a source of remorse for the captain. "Not like I was with my dad or my grandfather."

"Is he still around, your granddad?"

"He died of Boren's Syndrome when I was sixteen."

"I don't know what that is," Lessa admitted. "We didn't get much in the way of learning back home."

Rion gave her a sympathetic smile. "It's caused by the effects of war, exposure to radiation, certain gases, that kind of thing. Takes a toll . . . My grandfather was a marine, fought in the Insurrection, was away for long periods of time like my father. He was one of those larger-than-life types, you know? But Boren's, it ate at his mind and body." She met Lessa's gaze and gave a half-hearted smile. "He didn't regret it, though. Said it was his choice. He told me a lot of things in his final years. . . ."

"They'd be proud of you." At Rion's snort, Lessa frowned. "You don't think so?"

"Well, look around you. I didn't exactly follow in the Forge family footsteps. Instead, I'm trailing behind all their wars and battles, picking at the bones of their leftovers and selling salvage to their allies and their enemies. Honestly, I think they'd be appalled."

"Well, I think you're being too hard on yourself. You have a real nice ship, a good business, and you're not too bad a boss either."

Rion smiled. "Thanks."

"I know for a fact that if you hadn't picked us up, Niko would either be working the mines and probably sick by now, or he'd be lost in the guilds. You gave us a home. You didn't have to do that." Lessa chewed on her bottom lip, and once again focused intently on her fingernails.

"I'm glad to have you two on board." Rion's smile was sweet and grateful and caring, and Lessa wanted to crawl under the control panel. Her throat went thick. She'd always wanted someone to look at her like that—like they gave a damn—but now that someone had, it hurt, because it brought to the forefront the lack of any kind of love or attention she had growing up on Aleria.

"Is everything all right?" Rion asked.

Her defenses flared to the surface. "Sure, why wouldn't it be?"

Well, there it was. The perfect opening to *talk*. To finally gain more of a personal relationship with the captain. Lessa was burning inside, burning to tell someone about her past and the things that had happened to her back home, the horrible things she'd done to survive and to protect Niko. It was getting harder and harder to hold it in. . . .

And when the moment was right there in front of her, she panicked and turned coward.

"I don't know, you tell me." Rion countered with a curious tilt to her head, her dark eyes seeming like they could see every tiny horror on Lessa's conscience. "Is it Kip?"

Lessa blinked. "What?" Her face went hotter.

Rion let out a soft chuckle. "Never mind. Just . . . maybe don't go rushing into anything. There's time. Provided Kip doesn't jump ship, we're all going to be stuck together for a while. It's worth the time to get to know someone."

"Well, I don't . . . I mean, he's older. Not that I don't find him—ugh. Just shut up, Lessa." She covered her face with her hands and groaned. "I'm so embarrassed now." A light blinking on comms saved her from sinking into a deeper well of mortification. "I think this is for you," she said, noting Nor's call sign.

"You start asking around about a Covenant destroyer, and things might go bad for you," Nor said from behind her desk after Rion gave the Kig-Yar a vague summary of events on Eiro. "Trust me, I know. You might just"—she made an exploding motion with her claws, the sharp talons flicking outward—"disappear."

From the privacy of her quarters, Rion sat back in her chair and studied Nor's avian face. "Is that a threat, Nor Fel?" she asked, even though she knew it wasn't; she just liked to ruffle the old bird's feathers.

Nor's yellow eyes narrowed as she leaned closer to the screen. "Is fact. Dangerous times, you know this. Vestiges of the Covenant everywhere, pirates, smugglers, marauders . . . all want big guns. All searching the systems, building armies."

Rion paused, mulling over how she wanted to play this. "Eiro was a bust. I lost credits on this salvage—salvage *you* pointed me to, intel I paid good money for. It's not good business, Nor, giving bad intel."

The Kig-Yar leaned forward again, her beak nearly touching the screen, so close Rion could only see the outside corners of Nor's eyes. "*Rouse's* intel, not mine. And it was good. You found your scrap, no?"

"Found it and lost it. I paid you. *You* sent me to Rouse. I went on a pricey trip for zero return. I lost my grav carts and tools in the process. Someone sold away *my* intel." Rion's look turned calculating. Time to watch the fireworks. "Maybe I should just ask for my credits back."

As expected, Nor's shriek vibrated the speakers and her feathers shot straight up. The image wobbled, a blur of beak, plumage, and flashy accessories as the Kig-Yar's heavy fists slammed down upon the desk.

While Rion didn't think Nor or Rouse would've double-sold her intel, she wanted to get under Nor's skin, to light a fire and gain some information, if she could. And the number one thing that got under Nor's skin was having to dole out a refund. Once the Kig-Yar had even a single credit in her possession, giving it back was tantamount to torture.

"Look, I'll forgo the refund," Rion finally said, "in return for information. Good information this time."

Nor rearranged the glass beads hanging around her neck and righted a few shiny rings on her fingers. "Not dealing in destroyers. Already told you this."

"I don't *want* the destroyer. I want what's inside it. And it's not a weapon. You know me—I don't deal in the heavies. You do this for me . . . and I'll be in your debt for a change."

This seemed to make Nor very intrigued. "No refund?"

"No refund. I know your network has access to old Covenant intel, military history, records, transmissions. I want to know where the *Radiant Perception* ended up, if it was destroyed, where it was scrapped . . . anything at all."

Nor thought about it for a moment, and then bowed her head slightly. "Just this once, then. Next time you suck up your loss like a big girl, eh? I will be in touch." The transmission ended, leaving Rion without the opportunity for a comeback.

"Damn bird," she muttered, sitting back and biting her lip as she thought things through.

Radiant Perception couldn't have simply disappeared. A CPV-class heavy destroyer would have been an integral part of the Covenant fleet. Given the date, it was highly probable that the ship was part of the first wave of Covenant forces that had begun humanity's destruction with Harvest and continued on, creating as much devastation as possible. Any number of things might have happened to the vessel. But there should be a record or a mention somewhere; a ship that size didn't just fade into oblivion.

As Rion turned off her screen and sank back into her chair, she mentally prepared herself for the most likely scenario to come from all this: nothing. While the chances of finding out what had happened to *Radiant Perception* were decent, those of locating it intact and with the buoy still on board were astronomically low.

But then again, her dad always said Lady Luck was on their side. . . .

"One more, Daddy, please!" she begged with tears stinging her eyes. *But she wouldn't cry; she was tougher than that. He always called her his tough little lady, and she had to live up to the pride she saw in his eyes. Besides, crying always made him sad, always made that flash of guilt come into his eyes.*

And she never wanted her daddy to feel bad. Ever.

And especially not in the short amount of time they had together.

"All right, kid, one more. You deal."

She parked her elbows on the kitchen table and regarded him with a narrow look. "Loser deals."

He laughed at that, the lines around his eyes crinkling and his grin deep. She wanted to crawl over the table and throw her arms around him and beg him not to go. But she wouldn't.

So it was always one more game. As many more as he'd allow until he couldn't put off leaving any longer.

Once the cards were dealt, she grabbed her stack and faced her opponent. He was a big man, her father, with wide shoulders and scars and nicks all over if you knew where to look. Scrapes and cuts that marked every battle, every tour, every year away from her.

In his video messages home, he'd always show her the new ones. Some might think that would scare a child, make them even more worried. But for Lucy, it only proved how strong he was, how he came through every single time.

"War!" she cried, delighted as they turned over the same card and then spoke the rhyme. He won with an ace, looking pleased.

"See, told ya. Lucky card." He winked, flicking her on the nose with it.

"Take it with you, then." She wanted him to have all the luck he could get. She knew there was a war going on, a real one, not some game played at a kitchen table. She didn't know what it was about or why people were fighting, but she knew it was up there, way past the sky, where the stars lived.

"When you come home next, Momma says I'll be a big girl, maybe even double digits. You might not even recognize me."

He chuckled at that. "Have you looked in the mirror, kid?" Then he gave her a rare, serious look. Solemn. Emotional. "Me and you, we're a team. And a team sticks together, no matter the time or the distance. Don't for one second think I won't recognize you, Lucy O."

She loved it when he called her Lucy O. Never her entire middle name, Orion; just the O. It was special. Something only he did.

"Plus, we get to see each other," she reminded him, wanting him to feel better, to erase the sadness that had settled over him.

"Through messages, that's right. And you know I'll be sending you pictures of all the places I go."

And she'd have them printed and put in the scrapbook he'd bought for her.

They turned another set of cards.

And she had to bite her lip to stop the words that wanted to flood out of her mouth. Please. Don't go.

As he placed a card down, he held it there until she looked at him, sensing her struggle. "I love you, kid. Never forget that. I'll be fine. I'm good at what I do. It's in my blood. It's all I know, and it'll see me through and back here to you." He gave her a confident smile *that didn't seem to reach his eyes. "No need to worry, I've got Lady Luck on my side."*

He tucked the playing card, the ace she told him to keep, under his sleeve.

They turned their cards over onto the table again. "War," she said softly.

She won that time. And with each card turned, it felt like the clock on the wall counting down to him walking out the door.

"Hey," he said gently, reaching across the table to lift her chin. And she just couldn't hold it in any longer. Fat tears rolled from her eyes and her bottom lip quivered as she tried desperately to be strong and make him proud. "Aw, Loose, come here." He reached beneath her arms and brought her over the table until she was curled in his lap.

Her arms went around his neck and she held on tight, sobbing. How could she tell him how much she needed him when she didn't even know the words to say? Inside, her heart hurt and stretched like a balloon growing bigger and bigger until it might burst.

And then, inevitably, he was handing her over to her mother. He leaned in and kissed her mother's cheek, then joined his own father waiting by the door.

She watched him from the doorway, the sunlight nearly blinding her, so that all she could see was his outline moving down the walk and into the waiting car.

It was the last time she saw her father.

EIGHT

Ace of Spades, approaching Chi Rho comm sat

Niko was still running queries, intent on finding the tag, and coming up against a technology far beyond anything they'd come across before. Rion stood in the doorway to his quarters, the place a chaotic mess as usual—prints taped on the wall, notes haphazardly stuck on furniture and devices, clothes strewn on the floor . . . "If I told you to take a break, would you listen?"

He yawned, his eyes tracing across one of three monitors on his desk. "Probably not."

"We're coming up on Chi Rho. You'll have to table this once we're in range."

As she went to leave, he finally peeled his eyes from the screen. They were bloodshot and a little crazed. The kid was running on fumes. "We need an AI."

Not the first time he'd said so. And it wouldn't be the last.

"We have one."

"Yeah, a dumb one." He paused to take a drink from the bottle by his keypad. "Thing can only run systems. It can't find a tag. We need a smart AI. It would have found the tag the minute it was placed."

"You buying, kid? Because a smart AI is the cost of a damn ship, maybe more depending on the model and grade. Besides," she told him with a sweet smile, "*you're* my AI. And you didn't cost me a thing."

He rolled his eyes. As she left, she heard him mutter, "And I must be dumb too . . . dodgy little bastard doesn't want to be found."

"Take a break, Niko!" she called out while walking down the narrow corridor to the bridge.

There, Lessa was at comms scrolling through search results. She'd been at it for a few hours, mostly focusing on chatter, old accounts, and war stories, looking for any mention of the *Radiant Perception.* Kip was up from engineering and seated at the nav console, also glued to a screen and combing through archived military records. Cade was still in the hold, continuing work on the tracking system. He'd already used some of his old contacts to ask around discreetly about the destroyer and see if the name rang any bells, but it'd be a while before he got answers.

Rion sat in her chair as *Ace* settled into high orbit above Chi Rho. The comm sat was four thousand kilometers below them, give or take. Radar looked good. A small passenger vessel was on standard descent to the planet, and there was another heavy freighter in low orbit, unloading cargo onto smaller transports. Nothing out of the ordinary. Nothing emitting a signal similar to the one Niko had picked up from the stealth ship on Eiro.

Still, she kept *Ace* as dark as possible.

"Niko, we're in range."

"Fine. I'll patch you in from here," he answered over comms.

While Niko worked his magic, Rion pulled up her system logs and counted resources, noting how much food and drink was left in the dispensers, their water and oxygen reserves, and fuel cells.

"All right, you're in. Search away," Niko said.

They went to work, using the boost to reach into places and archives that might shed some light on the whereabouts of the *Radiant Perception*.

A solid hour went by and Rion's frustrations grew. "Anything?" she asked Kip and Lessa, even though she knew they'd tell her as soon as anything popped up.

Lessa turned slightly, chin parked in her hand, and shook her head. "Nothing. These old war accounts are really depressing, though."

"You'd think if the *Radiant Perception* was part of the first wave of Covenant that came through and started glassing planets," Kip said, "there'd be records of their progression, where they went before Arcadia and where they went after. But there are large gaps of time, discrepancies. . . ."

"Welcome to research hell," Rion said. "Glassed planets don't have good records, especially ones in the Outer Colonies. Good luck getting an accurate—"

"I found it! I found the little bastard!" Niko burst onto the bridge like some rabid Dwarkan squirrel. He glanced at them, eyes wide and blinking. He held a flat, square-shaped object in his palm, matte black and inconspicuous. "*I found it.*" The maniacal glee in his voice made Rion's brow lift.

"Boy, you've finally gone off the deep end," Lessa muttered. "Always said it was a matter of time. . . ."

Rion motioned him over. The tag was sleek and surprisingly heavy for as small as it was. "Where'd you find it?"

"In the aft landing-gear well. Cade helped me get it out."

Rion's temper flared as she placed the device back in Niko's hand, holding it there and looking the kid straight in the eye. "Eat something. Take a shower and a nap. Then I want you to pull the guts out of this thing and find out who made it tick."

"You're not going to destroy it?" Kip asked.

"It's salvage. Belongs to us now." Inside that small black square was a transmitter, and Rion intended to find out exactly who was on the receiving end.

"Rion, there's a message coming through from Nor," Lessa said. "Assuming you want to answer?"

"I do. Patch it through to my quarters. And Niko?"

"Yeah, boss?"

"After you're rested and back in the land of the living, I have a second job for you."

He frowned. "I want a raise."

Rion slid into her desk chair, turned on her display, and opened the blinking channel. Nor Fel's curved beak appeared so suddenly and so close that it gave Rion a start. Nor sat back, cackling.

"Real funny, Nor. You found something?"

Nor's humor evaporated. And Rion was surprised to note that the old bird actually seemed a little uncomfortable. Though, with the Kig-Yar, it was hard to detect subtle emotions—all those nuances and facial expressions that were so easy to read on the human face were much more difficult in many of the alien species.

Nor tapped her claws on the tabletop. The *tick, tick, tick* was unnerving.

Yeah, something bad was coming.

"The ship you look for, the *Radiant Perception*, crashed on Laconia in your . . ." She paused to look at something offscreen. "Sometime near the end of the time period you humans call *Febberry*—"

"February."

"Yes, or soon after that. Year twenty-five thirty-one." Rion's heart gave a bang. A tide of hope rose so swift and eager that she had to dig her nails into her palms, not wanting to give in to premature emotions. But, damn, the timing was right. It was *right*.

Options ran swiftly through her mind and one sequence of events seemed to rise above all the others. After a short skirmish with the *Roman Blue,* the *Radiant Perception* could have retrieved *Spirit of Fire*'s buoy. Sometime after that the Covenant destroyer must have met with resistance, or it could have been damaged from its run-in with the *Blue,* and crashed on Laconia. There might not have been enough time for the crew of the *Radiant Perception* to pass the buoy on to another ship or even for the Covenant to decipher the encryption themselves.

If this sequence proved true, and provided the buoy hadn't been destroyed during the crash, there was a very real chance that the *Spirit of Fire*'s buoy was indeed salvageable. The idea left chills running up her back.

"The ship has been on Laconia ever since," Nor continued. "It has never been lost. Just . . . avoided."

"Wait, what are you saying? There's salvage?"

"Yes. But it is infested." Nor's feathers ruffled. Whatever it was unnerved the Kig-Yar. "With Hunters."

A jolt of dread lifted the hairs on the back of Rion's neck.

Funny how one word could do that. *Hunters.* She stifled a shudder and tried to ignore her sinking hopes. "Any idea how many?"

Nor shook her head. "Word is there were many survivors after the crash. The Hunters, though, they kill whatever was left. Then they waited for rescue. None came, so . . . some say they multiply. Maybe true. Maybe whole ship, whole planet infested by now." Nor shuddered. "Me? Don't want to know. Can't confirm, of course . . . could all be talk. Rumor and more rumor. You know how that go."

The Mgalekgolo, or Hunters, as they were colloquially known, weren't like the Sangheili or the Kig-Yar. Once the Covenant War was over, many of them had engaged in a mass exodus to parts unknown. And humanity was very relieved about that.

It'd be an enormous hurdle dealing with Hunters, but first and foremost, they had to find the *Radiant Perception.* Rion would manage any other concerns when the time came. "Where's the likeliest place for a science station on a Covenant destroyer?"

"Depends. Lots of places."

"I mean a decryption center, a place for studying human technology. . . ."

"Bridge, most likely. They big places. Many stations and levels and ramps. Or somewhere close by. You got blueprints? I sell you some."

Rion smiled. "No. I'm all set, thanks."

"Now you owe *me*, Captain."

"Yes, I do. Thank you, Nor."

"One more thing." Nor's features went hard and serious. "Another salvage crew. Disappear." She made that exploding motion again by spreading her talons.

That got Rion's attention. "Which one?"

"Ram Chalva's. Last heard, they were on their way back from

digging under glass on Mesa. Had a couple old Kodiaks and a piece of Forerunner tech on board."

A sinking feeling settled in Rion's gut. Damn it. Ram Chalva was a pro, his salvage crew and his ship were top-notch. . . . The crews going missing in the last year just couldn't be coincidence. Someone out there was tagging salvagers, waiting for them to secure a payload, and then striking.

"Not good for business," Nor said. "Not good for any of us."

"Crews don't go missing without someone, somewhere talking about it." And there was so much traffic coming through the clearinghouse that Nor had to have heard inklings. Whispers. Talk. . . .

"There is one group of late," Nor admitted. "Unrulier than most. . . . Been gathering things up quick, been boasting, leader thinks he's beyond my rules. Name's Gek. Gek 'Lhar."

"Sangheili?"

"Worse. Sangheili commander. Some say he's part of a sect based on Hesduros, under Jul 'Mdama. Word is he's been sent out with a crew to secure weapons and ships. They organizing, growing, rebuilding the Covenant. Dangerous, that . . . dangerous for everyone."

And a creature like that with a holy doctrine fueling his every move wouldn't think twice about going after salvage crews, taking what he wanted, and calling it divine right. If it *was* this Gek 'Lhar . . .

"He is fight you can't win," Nor said perceptively.

Rion's grim expression became a flat smile. "You worried about me, Nor?"

"You flatter yourself, human. Worried about business."

"Where is he now, do you know?"

"I am not the first to inquire about your lost ship. Gek is

hunting for heavies. A destroyer would turn his head, no? Might be he's taken that ship by now."

"Understood. If you hear anything more about Gek, let me know."

"Will do, Captain." Nor gave a nod, leaned forward, and the screen went black.

Rion sat back, her thoughts churning. A ship infested with Hunters had been enough to keep salvagers at bay for at least a couple of decades. But these days, with ships and weapons at a premium and every faction out there desperate for power, there were those who wouldn't hesitate to face an infested planet if they thought the payout was great enough. If Nor was right and Gek 'Lhar had indeed beaten her to the *Radiant Perception*, Rion's search might end on Laconia. Or it might mean nothing at all.

The Hunter problem aside, she and this Sangheili commander weren't exactly looking for the same thing.

PART THREE

DOUBLE DOWN

NINE

Ace of Spades, 6 million kilometers outside the Procyon system

The *Ace of Spades* dropped out of slipspace at the edge of the Procyon system. Farther off course by several million kilometers than Rion would've liked, but not a bad spot given the fact that slipspace navigation was the definition of a shot in the dark. Destination points were never precise. Instead, they were viewed with a more general approach. If you arrived somewhere in or close to the vicinity you were aiming for, that was considered a successful jump in most travelers' minds.

Cade monitored Lessa's attempt at plotting a course correction to Laconia. Once achieved and entered, they began the journey at sub-light-speed.

Rion watched the interaction with a strange sense of detachment, her attention turning to the great canvas of black beyond the viewscreen and its handful of celestial objects. Tiny things. Just pinpricks of light. It felt odd to be there, moving through the system, following the same path as her father and the *Spirit of Fire.*

Like sailing in the shadows of giants.

"Less, put us within visual range of Arcadia," Rion said.

Ace maintained course for the next few hours and then swung aft by eleven degrees. Not long after, Arcadia emerged like a ghost from the darkness and dominated the viewscreen. A pale blue atmospheric ring circled the planet, creating a spectral glow around an otherwise ashen gray surface. No one spoke on the bridge. They all knew what they were looking at—a planet-size tomb. A grave marker of millions.

Rion had seen her share of glassed planets, and this one had been dealt a mortal blow. There were no pockets of color, no places where the ventral beams and their destructive plasma had not gone. It appeared the Covenant had been especially zealous in destroying this once resortlike human world.

Laconia, Arcadia's long-distance neighbor, hadn't received the same plasma bombardment, however. There was no colony to obliterate, no reason to pay mind to the cold, volcanic world. And while the planet could support life, the air was thin and harsh, the volcanoes mildly active and occasionally spewing sulfur dioxide. No need to bother with Laconia when the lush world of Arcadia was right around the corner and could serve as a better example of the Covenant's might.

Ace settled into low geostationary orbit roughly above the coordinates that Nor had provided. Somewhere below them on the rocky volcanic flows lay a Covenant destroyer. Rion pushed up from her chair and stepped to the main tactical table, which sat in the open space between the nav and comm stations.

"See if you two can pull up a decent image of the wreckage," she told Cade and Lessa. The volcanic ash in the atmosphere wasn't going to make it easy, but they could build a general image from the ship's lidar and quick mapping system.

Quelling her impatience, Rion waited, watching the display as a holographic image built.

"Looks like Nor was right," Cade said. "There's something living inside the ship. Picking up a large signal . . . Shit. Hold on." He paused. "There's more than one signal. We have eight outside of the *Perception* and a ship."

"Engaging baffling engines." Immediately Rion brought up a control panel, her fingers flying across the pad. "Run the sensors again, see if you can get a species match on those sigs." She turned to the tactical table and the holo-image. There was no need to ask about the ship Cade referenced. It was emerging right along with the massive destroyer. "Damn. It's a Covenant warfreighter. Older model. Fully-armed tithe ship. . . "

"There's still auxiliary power on the destroyer," Lessa said.

Now that was a surprise, a very good one. If there was still aux power, that meant there was a working power core. The damage down there might be minimal. The *Radiant Perception* could be a gold mine.

"The war-freighter's engines are powered down but hot," Rion said. "They just beat us, damn it."

"Eighty-seven percent probability that the eight outside the destroyer are Sangheili." Cade shook his head, annoyed. "Still working on the one inside. Next trip home, we're upgrading the life-detection software."

Yeah, she'd been meaning to do that.

Rion chewed on her bottom lip thoughtfully and stared at the two images hovering above the table. Her thoughts turned to the warning Nor had given her and the mention of the ex-Covenant commander, Gek 'Lhar. The war-freighter might have been dwarfed by the colossal destroyer, but it packed a punch with its heavy plasma cannon and two side-mounted turrets. And if that was Gek down there, he'd have not only firepower, but a wealth of tactical experience. Facing him wouldn't be easy.

Good thing she didn't plan to.

Cade joined her at the table and studied the destroyer image. "Looks like she's wedged in an old lava flow."

"And there's not much around to give us cover," Rion said, noting that, besides the Covenant war-freighter, the *Radiant Perception* was the lone anomaly on the landscape, a colossal hump in a large valley of cooled lava.

"No significant thermal readings from that volcano nearby. Environmentally, we should be good if we want to use those ridges." Cade pointed to an area of deep scores in the volcano's slope, which would provide decent cover. "It's three klicks from our target, but nothing we can't handle, provided those lava flats are stable."

Rion pulled up the destroyer's interior blueprints, placing them next to the lidar image. The area designated as bridge was enormous, several stories tall, with levels and stations and a network of elevators and ramps leading from one place to another. In the center of it all was a massive, raised central command.

"Niko, how are things coming on the detector?"

His voice came over the intercom. "She's just about ready, Cap."

"She?" Rion was almost afraid to ask. Niko had a habit of naming his toys.

"Yeah, I'm calling her Diane. She's loaded with every radio frequency and emergency transponder signal known to mankind. She can sniff out any UNSC signal on that ship. I added battery and energy emission signals too. If that buoy has a working power source, or even a decaying battery, my girl will find it."

"Nice work, kid."

"Thanks. Can I have that raise now?"

Rion bit back a smile and ignored him as she added the life detection intel to the blueprints and lidar to see exactly where each life sign was originating. "There." She pointed to the glowing red dot near the aft of the ship at the main entrance to the bridge, while eight more sigs were clustered inside the Covenant war-freighter.

"How about a bonus?" Niko said.

"Diane finds my buoy . . . then we'll talk."

"What are you thinking?" Cade asked her.

Rion scrutinized the images. "Well, ship's not infested . . ." The life detection scanner alerted on the lone signal within the destroyer. "Mgalekgolo. Ninety-two percent probability." Rion straightened and leaned against the table. "We could wait it out, let the Sangheili take care of the Hunter for us. They won't be looking for the buoy. They'll go for the heavy stuff."

"That could take them a long time, though. If the ship is as intact as we think it is, then there's months', maybe years' worth of salvage."

"Depending on what they're looking for. Won't take them long to scan for heavies, dropships, and if that *is* Gek 'Lhar down there, then I can bet you the first thing he'd look for is a luminary."

"Think so?"

She nodded. "If I were trying to rebuild the Covenant and out hunting for the best weapons and tech to help relaunch the war, I'd go for the single most precious thing on that ship. He'll look for the luminary first. Weapons and support ships second. You're right though—he might be there for a while, might call in reinforcements to help with the salvage."

"Which means we need to get inside that ship now," Cade said. "Before help arrives."

"We'll have to deal with the Hunter ourselves if need be and avoid the Sangheili. Hopefully, we can search for the buoy without either of them knowing we're there." She pointed to a damaged spot at the midsection of the ship, an area on the side opposite from where the Covenant war-freighter was parked. "We could enter there, then make our way to the bridge. . . ."

"The Hunter is on the bridge," Cade said. "I'm not sure we can avoid it."

Rion was already keying in a search and bringing up an image of a Hunter, placing it next to the destroyer's blueprints. The creature was almost four meters tall and weighed a stunning five tons. Covenant armor encased a colony of Lekgolo, orange eel-like creatures, which had bonded together physically and mentally to form a conscious, bipedal being. A Mgalekgolo. One of the handful of subspecies the Lekgolo were able to form, and the prime subspecies that the Covenant had put into action against humanity. A fuel rod cannon was integrated into the armor on one arm and the other held a two-ton shield as strong as a Covenant ship's hull.

"I'm the first to admit you're usually one lucky SOB, Forge, but getting in there, finding the buoy, and dealing with a Hunter if necessary—*without* being detected by the Sangheili . . . ?"

"And here I was thinking the odds weren't that bad. We've done some of our best work in stealth." They'd had plenty of experience in that particular area, after all. "I'm not worried about the Sangheili. The Hunter, though—that's the wild card." She glanced at Cade. "You've had contact with those things. Any insight?"

He stepped back and sat on the edge of the nav console. "Well, they're one of the tougher aliens to kill. Usually fight in pairs. If there's one down there, there's likely another. Depending on where it is on the ship, with aux power, and the ash in the atmosphere . . . we might not be picking up a second sig. Better to prepare for two of them."

Rion leaned over Lessa's shoulder to check the data again. "Well, it hasn't moved since we got here. And the signal itself, the energy that creature is putting off, is faint for its size."

"Signal might be faint for all kinds of reasons, Rion," Cade replied. "You know that. And one Hunter doesn't make the danger any less real. This thing probably doesn't even know the war's over, which makes it even more of a threat." He plowed his fingers through his hair, his manner becoming jumpy and bothered. "All it does is kill, Ri. It doesn't ask questions or try to communicate. I've seen them annihilate Covenant troops in the middle of battle just for stepping into their line of sight. That rumor Nor told you about started somewhere. There's a reason everyone has steered clear of the ship and why no one has attempted salvage."

"True. But that thing has been down there for twenty-six years," she countered, making sure her tone wasn't contentious. Obviously Cade's experience with the Hunters in combat had left some scars. . . . "It could be injured or dying or maybe even too old to fight. We can't say anything for sure, not until we check it out."

His response was an exasperated eye roll. "Well, if it's all the same to you, I'd rather not watch that thing rip you apart." He flung an arm toward Lessa. "Or any of us. Because that's what'll happen if it doesn't get you with its cannon. Don't think I haven't seen it done a hundred times before," he said, eyes hard and haunted. "You're not invincible, and you're being foolish if you think you can just walk in there without someone getting hurt." He pushed off the console and stormed off the bridge.

"I never said I was just going to *walk* in there . . . Cade!" she yelled after him, his assumption and attitude getting the best of her. She despised being walked out on in the middle of a discussion or a fight; Rion was a have-it-out-and-finish-it type of person. Things left unsaid, things unresolved . . . no. She had enough of that in her life already.

Annoyed, she placed her hands on the tactical table and leaned forward, her back to Lessa as she tried to regroup. She ran a hand over her face, then drummed her fingers on the table.

Cade was wrong. She preferred keeping her body parts intact, and she sure as hell didn't plan on waltzing right into that ship. "Well, I'm not giving up, that's for damn sure. We're right here. *Radiant Perception* is right below us."

Niko came onto the bridge and was immediately taken by the Hunter's image hovering over the table and completely oblivious to Rion's tension. "Hard to believe that thing is made up of worms." He shuddered and then checked the life sensor. "Huh. Pretty faint for its size. Maybe it's meditating." At Lessa's laugh, he gave an offended look. "What? I read it somewhere. Maybe you should try it sometime: you know, *reading.*"

"Okay," she said, rolling her eyes.

"Also I read they form pairs, like mates or brothers, and they're super tight. If one of them is killed, the other one goes nuts, like completely berserk. They feed on metals and alloys, so certain tech, circuitry, and infrastructure, are all possible meals, depending on what they like. . . . I'm not sure, but you think it might be able to sniff us out through our gear or through Diane?"

"Maybe," Rion said thoughtfully. "The destroyer still has power, though. Could be enough to sustain and feed that thing for years." No doubt the Covenant Empire had certain protocols in place to keep their Hunters from feeding on their tech. But the

Hunter had obviously found a way. To survive, you adapt. Unn Birger had told her that. Many times.

"Well, it could be bored eating Covenant tech. We might be like some new and delicious snack, and it'll come running like Lessa does every time you make brownies."

Behind them, Lessa snorted, then said, "Well, there's nothing on intel to suggest they like to snack on human tech. . . ."

"Why don't we just take it out?" Niko asked.

"Can't risk it, not until we know where the buoy is. We'd have to use cannons, grenades, or heavy fire to stop a Hunter. If we do, that'll alert the Sangheili, and alerting the Sangheili means my hunt for the buoy would be cut short. And that's not going to happen."

"Well, I kind of prefer staying in one piece. . . ." Lessa said.

Rion sighed and turned around so she could see both siblings. "You'll both stay here. This is a quick stealth grab. Hopefully we can avoid that Hunter and the Sangheili altogether."

"Assuming by *we*, you mean you and Cade," Niko said drily. He hated being left behind, but his talents were far too great to risk putting him in the field.

"The buoy won't retrieve itself. Cade and I will go in, start on the bridge, and use Diane to locate a signal. Once we know where the buoy is, we'll figure out the rest. . . ."

"Fine. You want me to system-check the av-cams? Been a while . . ."

"Yeah. Have Kip give you a hand." The last system check on the active camouflage units had been six months ago before a job on Shaps III. They were old units, traded by a couple of Zealots in return for half a dozen concussion rifles. The Zealots got the better end of the deal at the time, but over the long haul the av-cams had certainly earned out their initial loss.

"Once you turn Diane on and link up with me, your camo

will be compromised. We can scramble comms, make it look like static, but if someone is paying close attention . . ."

"Let's hope they're not and the scrap is keeping them distracted," Rion said, making her way off the bridge.

"Where are you going?" Niko asked.

"To check on Cade."

And she sure as hell hoped he'd cooled off by now, especially since she'd just volunteered him for a tour of the *Radiant Perception.*

Rion found Cade in his quarters, lying on his bunk, hands tucked behind his head and staring up at the ceiling. She sat on the mattress near his knee. "You know I have to go down there."

Always forward. Only forward.

His chest rose and fell with a deep sigh. He pulled his attention from the ceiling. "I know. You're incredibly transparent when it comes to things you want."

At her eye roll, he rose onto his elbows until they were eye level and laid it all out. "You're going in dark. You'll check things out. Make a beeline for the buoy and then improvise your way out." A lopsided smile pulled at one corner of his mouth, but his eyes were worried and still annoyed.

"Your point?"

"We've been crewing together for six years. We play our little games, you and me. Take what we want from each other, dance around any kind of future or possibilities . . ."

As Cade tried to find the right words to continue, Rion realized that he'd summed up their relationship with a few simple sentences, words that sounded so easy and maybe even a little empty. But they weren't. At times, she'd had similar thoughts. Wanted possibilities, wanted to admit feelings, admit loneliness and fears, and look to a committed future together. But the places they went to, the people they dealt with, the risks of space travel . . . Rion didn't like to lose or hurt or contemplate the possibility of future losses.

And neither did Cade. He'd already lost his family, a wife and two children. Parents and siblings. He didn't want to lose again, and especially not to some crazy-ass undertaking on a wrecked destroyer with, of all things, a Hunter on board.

She understood.

But she was still going down there. And he damn well knew it.

Cade returned to staring once more at the ceiling with a tic in his jaw. "I've been thinking about the first time we met, when Sorely threw you against the bulkhead."

She smiled at the memory. "I never hit the bulkhead." Because Cade had been lined up there with the rest of the crew, watching in the cargo hold of Birger's ship, and she'd plowed right into him. He'd boosted her up and whispered in her ear: *Old left shoulder injury. Knees are bad too.* Then he'd pushed her toward the fight with a smack on the ass. It had shocked her so much that she'd glanced back at him, surprised by his audacity, and when she turned back to the fight, Sorely's fist met her face. She dropped like a stone, the world spinning. Slowly, she'd rolled to her belly and pushed up to see Cade wincing apologetically. And then she'd gone for Sorely's knee and then his shoulder.

She won that fight because of Cade.

It had been a shifting point in her status on the ship and in her career to follow.

"You trying to tell me I can't win this fight?" she asked.

His brow lifted and he nudged her thigh with his knee. "No, Forge. I'm telling you I've got your back. Like always."

Her chest expanded a little, an uncomfortable pressure building there, full of regrets and wonderings and possibilities. "Good," she said, then cleared her throat. "Now tell me how you think we should deal with this Hunter."

TEN

Surface of Laconia, Procyon system

The oxygen on Laconia was thin, but not enough to warrant a suit and tank. All they needed to add to their wardrobe were jackets for warmth, and instead of tanks on their backs, they carried weapons and the active camouflage units that would render them nearly invisible as they approached the destroyer. Cade, with his rifle at the ready, walked beside Rion over the lava flats, a sack of grenades strapped to his back and two on his belt. There was a harsh nip to the temperature and a sting in the nose from the sulfur in the air. *Ace* lay three kilometers behind them, nestled in the dugout of two volcanic ridges.

"Keep an eye on those Sangheili," Rion reminded Lessa over comms.

"Will do, Cap."

Rion wasn't too concerned. Gek, if it *was* him, wouldn't be dedicating resources to looking for life signs or scanning the area with any real intensity. He'd be more concerned with the Hunter in the ship and finding his loot. Gek was more a worry to them if they had to engage the Hunter, and by doing so, alert the Sangheili to their presence.

"You ever kill a Hunter, Cade?" Niko asked over comms.

"Nah. Jackals, yeah. And Grunts. A *lot* of Grunts. But no . . . no Hunters. Not directly anyway."

"Ever see one killed?"

"More than enough, I suppose. Rocket launchers usually got 'em. Trick is to hit them in the waist area, in their soft, unprotected parts."

"How about an Elite? Have you killed one of those?"

"Yeah, a few . . ."

"Ever see a Spartan?"

Static, and the crunch of their footsteps over hardened lava, filled the ensuing silence as though the entire galaxy paused to acknowledge the word. These were the things that Cade never really talked about. Spartans were the stuff of legend, human civilization's biggest, baddest soldiers. Everyone had heard the insane tales, the near mythological feats. They'd watched grainy footage, read firsthand accounts in the news and on forums, seen images caught on camera and put on chatter, or sanctioned clips released by the military. . . .

"A time or two," Cade answered.

"And?"

He remained quiet. Thinking. Remembering.

"Well, kid . . . they're everything people say they are and more. Bigger than you expect, more agile than you expect, and if you thought they were badasses before, when you see them in action, that word doesn't even come close. They can do things that would blow your mind. Sometimes you had to wonder if they were more machine than human. . . ."

Cade's words settled into the radio silence; the only sound once more was the *crunch, crunch, crunch* of their boots on the ground.

"Kip, how's that Hunter looking?" Rion asked.

"Hasn't moved."

"Less?"

"All eight sigs are still on board the war-freighter."

"Diane's got a location radius of half a klick, so once you get into the ship, just give me the all clear and I'll turn her on," Niko said.

As they drew closer to *Radiant Perception*, the true measure of the vessel's scope and size was astonishing. She was held tight by the grip of the lava field. A good third of the bow's bulge was buried along with the repulsor engines at the stern, while the upper portion of the midsection lay exposed. But it was the two visible wings that caught Rion's attention the most. They curved up from the stern like the giant tusks of some fallen alien behemoth. Beneath the volcanic dust and ash, the sleek curves still held a lavender sheen despite the years; the nanolaminate alloy had never rusted, never faded. . . .

It looked as though she'd simply sunk in lava and couldn't get out, her exotic skin able to withstand the intense heat. Though due to the crash, the lava would have seeped into holes and cracks, filling up volume, and cooling into natural grappling hooks, holding the ship in place.

"Radiation levels are good," Rion said, noting her readout. "Must have shut down the fusion reactors." The more she studied the wreck, the more certain she became that the landing had been a somewhat controlled descent.

They continued, passing under the shadow of the destroyer, like ants marching around a sleeping dinosaur. There were a few jagged openings on the hull, some from the landing, but the rest obviously the result of enemy fire.

"Rion." Cade gestured to the opening they'd seen on the holo-image, a massive hole blown in the hull right behind the midsection's convergence with the bow. "Something that size . . . had to be a MAC."

Rion stopped and regarded the enormous hole. Then she stepped past Cade, giving him a grin and a pat on the shoulder as she went. "Well, that's awfully nice of the UNSC, leaving us a door and all."

"We always did aim to please," he drawled from behind her.

Rion paused at the entrance and studied the blueprints once more in relation to the hole in front of them and committed to memory the best path to the bridge.

"All right, kids, we're inside. Going comm dark," she quietly told the crew. Once she acknowledged their replies, Rion shut down her link.

The MAC rounds had done an impressive amount of damage on the inside of the ship, where mangled conduits, cables, and fiber optics lay strewn among the ruins of interior bulkheads, decks, and infrastructure. Once Rion and Cade oriented themselves and saw beyond the wreckage, finding a passageway in the right direction was no trouble—a tight squeeze through a bent bulkhead, and then they were on their way to the bridge.

The ship was a maze of dark-lavender-tinted metal, open decks, twists and turns, ramps and access bridges over vast spaces. A few dead ends from closed bulkhead doors cost them some time. In areas that held little damage, the interior lighting was still on, casting the corridors in an eerie violet glow. But what struck her the most was the number of casualties. Hiking through an immense ship strewn with the remains of long-dead Covenant was a first. She stopped counting the times they came across Hunter remains or stepped over groups of skeletons still wearing their armor, still holding weapons . . . and she had to wonder if their deaths were the result of the crash or if they were all victims of the surviving Hunters on board.

When they passed over the deck above a large shuttle bay, Rion knew they were getting close. "The salvage on this thing could feed us for decades," Cade said as he climbed over a dislodged console, pausing at the top to reach back and grab Rion's hand. As their hands connected, he laughed. "Or at least spring for Niko's raise."

"Thank God he's not seeing this or I'd never hear the end of it. Kid's due, but I'm waiting for him to go one day without asking. *One* day . . ."

"Tyrant," Cade said.

She grinned.

As they descended the other side of the debris and continued, Rion studied the dropships and support vessels still anchored in the bay below. "I don't see any damage on those."

"Me either. Looks like any of them would fly with little or no repair."

What really astounded her was that all this tech and surplus had been sitting here for more than two decades—a known and documented site in certain circles, and no one in those circles had come calling. The fear of the Hunters—or the mere rumor of them—had made this site a true treasure trove. And Rion wanted to keep the rumor intact, because she had every intention of coming back for more.

They continued up an access ramp. Ahead was a large

opening, one that the blueprints marked as leading directly onto the bridge. Cade paused and motioned for them to stick close to the wall. Rion moved to the bulkhead, relieved the blast doors weren't closed, and eased quietly along with Cade in front, knowing that whatever was causing the weak life sign lay somewhere beyond.

Near the entrance, Cade stopped, met Rion's gaze, and then gave a quick nod before ducking his head around the door in a fast, efficient manner. He pointed to the right, indicating caution in that direction. Then he disappeared around the left corner.

Rion followed his lead, but her attention stayed right where a large lump of metal lay in a deep corner.

Hunter.

Its massive two-ton shield lay discarded on the floor along with a fuel rod cannon nearby. There were open places in its body armor where the Lekgolo worms could be seen. But there was no movement. No outward sign of life.

They moved away from the doors, backs pressed against the wall until they came to a bend and found cover there. Behind them lay a second lump of armor—another Mgalekgolo, this one dead, given the dried-up bits of brown-orange flesh clinging to the metal and spread out on the floor.

So there *had* been a pair.

Rion leaned against the wall, allowing herself a moment to regroup. The dead Hunter, the weak signal of the one that remained—one that had possibly lost its bond brother—all came together to suggest that perhaps she and Cade had gotten very, very lucky. Because from her viewpoint, the Hunter in the corner didn't appear to be a danger, it appeared to be dying.

Cade's trigger finger tapped on the side of his rifle. He wanted to kill it, now, while it was vulnerable. After getting his attention,

Rion shook her head. His eyes narrowed to fine angry points and his mouth went tight.

Despite her obvious reluctance to fire her weapon and alert the Sangheili, executing a living creature that posed no threat, no matter what it was, wasn't part of Rion's bag of tricks. She had *some* scruples. Cade, however, obviously disagreed, his expression saying he had every right to cut down the hostile, sleeping or not. To him, that Hunter represented the brutal slaughter of hundreds of his fellow soldiers. . . . It was still the enemy, and for a part of Cade, the war would always rage on.

When Rion motioned her desire to start the search, he declined, indicating he was staying put to keep an eye on the beast. She wasn't surprised. "I'm going to take a look around before activating Diane."

Rion moved away and got her first good look at the bridge. Seeing a control room so elaborate and alien made her wonder how the hell they'd ever survived the war at all. With ships like these, and the technology the Covenant wielded . . . it was a miracle and a testament to humanity's will and strength that they'd emerged from the onslaught. Bruised and grieving, yes, but still intact.

The command area rose from a thick column in the center. Several ramps around the space led up to stations and platforms, decks where, in the past, one could access the light bridge that led to the central hub.

Rion started checking each station, looking for anything that appeared out of place. The bridge had sustained minimal damage—not enough to account for all the casualties in her path. She tried to put the gruesome sights behind her and focus on checking counters, corners, any place the buoy might have rolled or fallen or been stashed.

It had been relatively easy to remain hopeful before. Every clue leading her to this moment had felt like fate was guiding her hand. But after two hours went by, she began to lose faith.

Another ten minutes, and she headed back to Cade and the immobile Mgalekgolo. Cade was leaning against a console, rifle lying across his lap. His gaze lifted when he heard her approach. "Any luck?" he asked quietly.

"Nothing."

He read her frustration easily. "You want to break silence."

"I want that goddamn buoy."

As she pulled Diane from her pack, Cade straightened and trained his rifle on the Hunter. Without preamble, Rion switched the device on, then lifted her arm, activated comms, and said just above a whisper: "Niko, Diane is up. You read?"

"Got her, boss." His voice rang out loud and clear, making them both wince and train their attention on the Hunter, but it showed no reaction at all. "You're good to go. And . . . hot damn, you owe me that bonus, cuz my girl is already singing. Keep walking and I'll direct you."

Rion left Cade to guard the Hunter and moved around the perimeter of the bridge. Niko corrected her a few times and finally, after several minutes, they found a corridor leading off the bridge, Diane pinging hard.

There were rooms on each side, and a few meters in, Niko told her to stop and move right, then: "Left. Definitely left."

Rion squeezed through a tight spot in a damaged bulkhead, coming out into a large room that appeared to be some sort of secondary communications center.

"You're close, boss. Signal is right in front of you."

Rion scanned the room. Sleek counters, consoles, tables . . . There was some minor damage, mostly near the door. Cabinets were askew, panels buckled and cracked, a few tables overturned. As she went straight ahead, she studied every aspect she came into contact with, but all of it looked alien, Covenant. There was nothing that shouted UNSC. Her last hope was at the far wall of cabinets, which stretched the length of the room and appeared to be workstations of some sort.

Not finding anything on the countertop, she dropped to one knee and ran her hand over the sleek, flat fronts of the counter. Suddenly, a panel gave way. A door popped open.

And there it was. An unassuming gray ball of alloy amid a tangle of alien hardware.

For a moment, she couldn't move. All she could do was stare with broken breath and stunned mind at the buoy nestled in its prison for the last twenty-six years. She rubbed her face and let out an uneven exhale as a slow electric shock slid along every nerve, branching out until it tingled her fingertips. History. She was looking at history. A solid, physical link to the *Spirit of Fire*.

A link to her father.

"Talk to me, boss."

She jerked at the sound of Niko's voice.

"Boss?"

Rion cleared her throat. It was thick with emotion. "Niko?"

"Yeah?"

"Consider that raise a done deal."

His whoop cut through some of her shock and she found herself grinning and feeling rather breathless. "I'll see you back on the ship."

"Cha-ching. Roger that. See you soon."

Rion's hands were trembling as she took care to untangle the buoy from the cabinet's contents. It was heavy and cold, and utterly priceless.

Once it was secure in her pack, she pushed to her feet, hiked the bag over her shoulder, and made for the break in the bulkhead, reminding herself to stay focused. They weren't in the clear yet.

As she exited the room, emerging back into the corridor, she became disoriented. The bridge opening should be there, to her right, but there was nothing but a wall of darkness.

Wait. This wall was . . . breathing?

No. *Writhing.*

The hulking mass made a step toward her.

Rion stumbled back as the Mgalekgolo straightened to its full height.

Fear snaked down her spine. The holo-image had not done it justice at all. There was no two-ton shield, no cannon. Just body armor and wormy hands that could grab and rip as Cade had warned. Spikes jutted out of its back and shoulders, but they were limp and bent to one side.

Rion continued to back away, pulling her rifle over her shoulder and flicking the safety off. The Hunter's orange belly and neck were exposed, its arms out wide as though daring her to strike.

A strange vibratory groan radiated from the creature, a peculiar, deep sound. A low, keening wail that seemed more in her mind than outside in the corridor. Though that wasn't possible, was it? As the sound threaded around her, a deep sense of loneliness and grief filled her up and left her utterly stricken.

"End."

She wasn't sure if she heard that word outright or if it somehow had sprouted directly into her mind. Tears stung her eyes and she felt like she was drowning in the creature's grief.

What the hell?

The Hunter made an aggressive step forward and suddenly slammed its fists together. It stomped a massive foot, egging her on.

"*End.*"

But she couldn't make herself shoot. Something was off. It didn't feel right.

A *thwack, thwack, thwack!* of shots rang out. Rion jerked, the sudden, unexpected barrage piercing her eardrums. Orange sprayed in an arc from the Hunter's opposite side. She felt that moan again in her mind, that hurt and loss and desolation. The pain.

And above all, the relief. The staggering relief.

The Hunter turned toward Cade, stomping again as though about to charge him.

Thwack, thwack, thwack!

She flinched each time, ears ringing, eyes stinging, her throat growing thick with emotions that felt very real, yet irrational at the same time.

The Hunter doubled over as orange matter and liquid dropped to the floor, and fine bits splattered the wall beside her, a few landing on her chin and cheek.

The Hunter fell. And as it did, she continued to experience its pain and its relief.

"Rion!" Cade shouted.

Dazed, she couldn't find her voice. In the back of her mind, she knew they had to get the hell out of there. There was no way the Sangheili outside would've missed the commotion.

"Rion!"

"I'm here. I'm fine."

Cade edged around the dying Hunter, weapon still trained. "I'm sorry," he said, breathing heavy, tripping over the words.

Rion pulled her focus from the creature and saw that his hands were trembling. His skin was white and his pupils dilated. A small line of blood ran down his temple.

"Are you hurt?"

He blinked. "What?"

"You're bleeding."

"No. I—shit. My head."

Rion touched his shoulder and he nearly jumped out of his skin. "Cade," she said carefully. "What happened?"

A flush appeared on his pale face. "Jesus, Ri, you could have died. And I—I choked is what happened."

She reached out again, but he flinched, moving away in shock.

"It stood up. The Hunter . . . and I just froze."

"You're bleeding. Let me—"

He knocked her hand away and let out a sharp, crazy laugh. "Yeah. Not only did I choke, but I fell ass over end on some goddamn piece of debris and knocked myself out."

"It's oka—"

"*It's not okay!*" he roared, eyes turning glassy. "Damn it, Rion! It's *not* okay! It only came looking for you because I took myself out of play!"

And then he was storming away, leaving her alone and still trying to process everything that had just happened. She stared at the dead Hunter, wondering if what she'd heard and felt had been real. It *had* come looking for her—a second option after Cade had fallen.

But it had done so because it wanted to die. She was sure of it. It had left an unconscious Cade and found her to do the deed instead.

Maybe there was some truth to what Niko had said about bonded pairs. . . .

"Uh, Cap? Those sigs are on the move, entering the ship now. You have plenty of time to get out, but you've got to go now."

"Copy. We're headed out."

Leaving the creature behind, Rion ran after Cade.

He was already moving off the bridge. "Cade!" she yelled after him.

Rion hesitated as she passed the center column that supported the bridge's central command hub. Somewhere up there, a luminary might very well still be intact. . . .

She glanced down the path Cade had taken and then back up at the column. The buoy was in her possession, her partner was already gone, and she wasn't about to press her luck.

Down the familiar passageways, she hurried after Cade. To the hole in the hull. And finally back onto the lava flows, breathing the thin, sulfur-laced air, and away from the ship.

Once *Ace* came into view, Rion's patience gave way. She caught up to Cade and grabbed his arm. He spun on her. His color was back and his pupils were no longer the size of dinner plates, but his eyes held a wealth of horror, guilt, and embarrassment— emotions she rarely saw in the ex-marine.

"Cade . . . wait. It's not your fault."

He laughed and kept walking. "Why? Because I have *history*? That doesn't give me a free pass to spaz out on you like that."

"Yeah. Actually, I think it does." He wasn't a Spartan, for God's sake. He was just a man.

He stopped. "No, it *doesn't*. Not for me." Disgusted, he continued on, but then changed his mind, turning around to face her. "You know how many times I found myself *this close* to a Hunter? More times than I can count. I'm talking Mgalekgolo in their prime. Not some weak-ass lumbering old worm farm without any shield or weapons. And when do I decide to choke?"

"Cade . . . you haven't seen a Hunter in eight years. *Eight years*. So what, you froze. I'm fine. I didn't need your protection. Stop taking on that responsibility—I never asked you to." He flinched as if she'd struck him. It was an unfair blow and she instantly regretted her words. He'd been saving her the moment he helped her beat Sorely. And, yeah, she never asked him to then either. But it was part of who he was, part of what they did for each other.

He shook his head, some of his emotions appearing to deflate as he continued on to the *Ace of Spades*. "Doesn't matter."

"Yes, hell, it does."

"No," he said as she drew up next to him, matching his pace. "It really doesn't."

"Fine. Let me know when you learn to give yourself a god-damn break."

And with that, she jogged ahead of him.

ELEVEN

After boarding *Ace* and debriefing the crew, Rion sat on the ship's loading ramp, arms resting over her knees, staring out at the gray volcanic world and the destroyer in the distance, curious as to why the Sangheili had given up the chase so easily. Surely, and with the wealth of tech aboard the *Radiant Perception*, they had enough experience to track their position. Yet they'd called off the pursuit almost before it had begun.

The sulfur wind blew her hair around her face. She tucked it behind her ears and watched the powder-fine ash blow across the flats. If ever there was a place that fit the definition of *alien*, Laconia was it. And though she'd seen plenty of beautiful planets, it was those like Laconia that always held her interest and got her wanderlust pumping. If there was salvage in the mix, even better.

A war of irritation and guilt was making the rounds inside her. She was pissed at Cade for being so unyielding with himself. And she was pissed with herself for making that shitty comment to begin with.

Truth was, he'd saved her ass too many times to count. In the early days of running the *Hakon*, she'd been something of a renegade. She loved taking risks, laughing in the face of insurmountable odds, and even loved a good, bruising fight that left her stiff for weeks. She was by no means the roughest salvager out there, but luck and a little skill had seen her through. There'd been some crazy sons of bitches, though . . . most of them dead now. Some of them so out-of-this-world violent that they gave the average marauders and pirates a bad name—she could think of a certain Brute and his cronies who fit that description very well. The group was so vicious they'd been banished from the Covenant back in its prime. How she'd like to put their leader six feet under and watch him work his way through a thousand levels of hell, but unfortunately he was still on the move, cutting a swath of red through the galaxy.

Sometimes Rion wondered if Cade hadn't come along where she'd be now. . . .

Footsteps over metal rang out, and vibrated through the ramp. Cade sat down beside her, feet straight out and hands braced behind him. He was quiet for a while, watching the plume from an unseen volcano far in the distance and the small clouds of ash picked up by the wind and sent spinning over the lava flows.

"Messed-up day."

Rion snorted. "Yeah."

"Found your buoy, though."

"Unbelievable, huh?" She couldn't help the frown. "Doesn't seem real. It's been, I don't know . . . almost too easy."

Cade chuckled. "It took you twenty-six years to find a good lead, Forge. That ain't easy. Things are just snowballing right now." He bumped her with his shoulder.

"Still a long ways to go . . ."

A particularly large swirl built and they watched it dance across the landscape until it dissipated.

"Look, I'm—"

"What I said—"

They stopped in unison. Rion laughed. And then: "You don't have to say anything. What I said back there . . . It was ungrateful and—"

"Right," he finished. "It was right. You've never needed saving. You never asked me to. Granted, without me around, you might be missing a few fingers and limbs by now, maybe a ship or two, but you'd have made it through without me."

"Smart-ass."

"You've saved me too. A dozen times over."

He bumped her with his shoulder, before letting out a weary breath. "Can't believe I froze . . . And for God's sake, don't tell the crew. I'll never live it down." He smiled halfheartedly, while deep disappointment lurked in his eyes. It'd be a long time before Cade could make this right with himself. "I'm getting old, Forge. Old and scared."

She rolled her eyes. "The day you get old and scared is the day I berth this ship for good."

Cade cocked his head, gaze narrowing on her, searching as though he was weighing an important decision. Then he gave a casual, offhanded shrug. "I suppose I could retire with you."

A slow grin spread across her face and her heart tripped. "I suppose I could too."

A *thud* echoed behind them, followed by whispers. Glancing over their shoulders, they saw Lessa and Niko perched on the catwalk, two eavesdropping cretins, grinning like damn fools.

"Hey, boss!" Niko called. "With my raise I think I might retire with you too." Then he had the *nerve* to make kissing noises.

"God, that kid has the most amazing lack of self-preservation." Cade met Rion's gaze as the siblings giggled from the catwalk.

"I'm going to kill them."

He flashed her a wide smile. "Not if I do it first."

Cade was up and running, Rion hurrying after him. When Niko saw them coming, he shrieked like an adolescent Jackal, the high-pitched sound making Rion stop and double over in laughter. Lessa's laughing scream followed Niko's, ringing out over the cargo hold as they hightailed it off the catwalk, Cade taking the steps two at a time, the metal ringing with the force.

Old and scared, my ass.

"Cap?"

Rion paused on the stairs at the sound of Kip's voice over comms. "There's a life-form running across the flats. Scan says it's human."

She went still. Cade and the others began to quiet down.

Rion hurried to the locker room, grabbed a pair of high powered binoculars, and ran back to the loading ramp. "Direction?" she asked.

"Heading east from the war-freighter."

Rion trained her sights on the ship and then tracked east. What she saw chilled her to the bone. "Jesus. That's Ram Chalva."

And he was running for his life.

His clothes were ragged. Blood and dirt covered his exposed skin. He was barefoot and struggling.

She tracked back to the Covenant war-freighter and her blood went cold. A large gray-skinned Sangheili was aiming at Ram. She knew that combat harness he wore, had even sold a few a couple of years ago. It was the kind once worn by the rank-and-file Sangheili in some of the Covenant's first-wave assault lances. His head was bare, a bulky mass with parallel ridges protruding down the back of his skull to his thick neck. He was taller than the others taking shots at Ram, and held an air of authority. Something flashed on his shoulder, but she couldn't see what it was. But she knew one thing—this wasn't a pursuit. It was target practice. And what better way to flush out the other meddling salvagers here than to use another human for bait?

"Well, now we know why they gave up so easily," Rion murmured. Then, "Cade, get up to the bridge. Kip, lay down fire until Cade gets there."

"Now?" Kip asked.

"Yes, now! Right now!"

Rion raised the ramp a meter off the ground and then left it open, waiting only long enough to see a line of fire from *Ace*'s cannon split the atmosphere and connect with the destroyer behind the Covenant war-freighter. "The war-freighter, Kip!" She ran up the stairs with a mental note to never put Kip on weapons. "Cade, hurry the hell up!"

A minute later, Rion burst onto the bridge as *Ace* lifted off.

"I'm taking control." She slid into her chair. "Kip and Niko, get down to the loading ramp. We're going in for a scoop."

Rion engaged thrusters. *Ace* surged forward, gaining speed, then banking hard left toward Ram Chalva's position. "Less, where is he?!" Rion shouted as a plasma bolt shot over their bow. Lessa was up and looking. . . .

"There!"

Rion zeroed in, flying *Ace* low to the ground and right over Ram's head. She banked hard again and set *Ace* down ahead of him so that all the fleeing salvager had to do was run up the damn ramp. If he could. "Niko, Kip, do you have him?"

Confirmation seemed to take forever.

Another shot slammed the ridge beyond them. Ash rained down and the ship shook from the blast.

"We got him! Go, go, go!"

"Hold on!" Rion gave everything to thrusters and *Ace* shot into the sky. Once the ramp was closed and the air lock engaged, she activated shields. Then she banked the ship again. She wasn't running. She wanted payback. Cade glanced over his shoulder. She met his gaze. "Bring the autocannons around and target that ship."

The Covenant war-freighter was too close to the *Radiant Perception* to drop a missile. Rion had every intention of coming back to Laconia and picking that destroyer apart. Damaging it now wasn't in the cards.

He nodded and turned back to weapons controls.

The war-freighter was lifting off.

"Three more ships!" Kip shouted. "What the hell?"

"From the destroyer," Rion said tightly. "They're using *Perception*'s dropships." Which meant they had a small army at their disposal. "Cade?"

"Firing now. . . ."

Ace screamed over the war-freighter as the cannons let loose, but a quick maneuver from the ship caused only minor damage to its wing. Enemy fire began to rain down on them.

Damn it. Reluctantly, Rion pulled *Ace* up and headed for the stars.

TWELVE

Ace of Spades, 32,000 kilometers from Laconia

Checking File Systems..... DONE...
Checking Security...... DONE...
>>>>>>>>>>>>>>
ONI FIELD PAD
LOG IN: ********
PASSWORD: *************
>>>>>>>>>>>>>
Encryption Code: OCTWTF
Clearance Level: H
ACCESS GRANTED

To: Hahn
From: 67159-021127

Location: Laconia / Procyon system
Found: CPV-class heavy destroyer, *Radiant Perception*, crash-landed on the surface of Laconia. Mostly intact.
Recovered: Log buoy dropped from UNSC *Spirit of Fire.*
Current: . . .

The cursor blinked as Kip paused and wondered what the hell he had gotten himself into.

He'd just left the lounge after dinner with Niko and Lessa. They'd found not only the buoy but also saved the life of a well-known missing salvager. Rion and Cade had spent most of their time in the med bay providing medical attention. But dinner was a positive affair once they returned with news that Ram Chalva would make it. What followed was a rousing, good-natured debate, interesting conversations, laughter, even a few games of Alerian dice—courtesy of Lessa and Niko.

And now Kip was selling everyone out.

He was in over his head, something of which he was well aware. If he was honest with himself, he'd known it the moment Agent Hahn had approached him on Sedra eight months ago.

After the terrorist attack there, with a bioweapon that had destroyed countless lives, he'd tried to go back to work and had lasted a few weeks, going through the motions, making reports on autopilot until it was too overwhelming to get up and go out anymore, until he had to face reality—the shattered and irreversible world he'd found himself in.

And once reality had come calling, he hadn't been able to go back to the way things were, instead falling into a deep depression that no amount of artificial means or grief counseling would help.

Though Cade didn't know it, he and Kip shared something

in common. Kip had lost everyone too. His sister, his younger brother, his brother's family—nieces and nephews . . . and Talia. Talia with her thick red hair and loud mouth. Talia with her crazy ideas and inexhaustible lust for life. Black had crept through her veins like a wave of spiders on the march, scattering, scurrying, dividing and laying down a pattern of inky webs. Black-patterned abdomen, six months along, and inside, black-patterned baby . . . The stuff of nightmares.

He'd finally snapped.

And proceeded to drink himself into a stupor on the floor of the baby's room. A room his child would never see. The rocking chair his wife would never sit in. The books they'd never read there together.

That room was broken now too, destroyed in his grief.

He'd been enraged at his inability to help, or do a damn thing about anything. Sedra had gone through the war and come out the other side. They'd actually made it. And then to be subject to a terror attack by Sangheili Zealots that killed so many people? It wasn't right. It wasn't fair. And it ate away at him like the black poison that had killed his family.

The chime at the door came, first one day, then two, then three, again and again, relentlessly until he rolled his body off the sofa, pulled his drunken self off the floor, and staggered to the door, throwing it wide.

He couldn't have been more confused at the sight of three identical men standing in the doorway. "Silas Kipley?" they asked.

He blinked several times until three turned into two and finally two into one. He braced his hand on the doorframe and shook the fog from his brain. "Who's asking?"

"I'm Agent Hahn with the Office of Naval Intelligence. May I come in?"

"Look, I already gave my report to the SCG. Everything is in there." And even through his stupor, he remembered that he'd done one hell of a forensics job on that Bactrian-class tug, the one that had smuggled the raw material used to make the bioweapon that had killed his family. He'd been focused, determined, had been able to use his knowledge to do some good and ignore what he'd lost. At least for a little while. He went to shut the door, but Hahn's hand shot out.

"Mister Kipley, this isn't about your report." Hahn looked more businessman than ONI agent. He had a slight build, a kind face, and a balding head. His eyes went narrow and assessing as he took in Kip's appearance. "Have any idea what day it is, Mister Kipley?"

"Couldn't care less. So if you don't mind, I have a sofa calling my name."

He went to shut the door again, but Hahn stopped him. Again. Anger stirred in Kip's gut, replacing the sour bite and bitterness that usually held sway. He went to tell the guy to get lost, but Hahn spoke first.

"We can make it so what happened to you doesn't happen to someone else, some other family, some other child. . . ."

Before he even had a chance to recognize the emotion, it was there, stinging his throat and filling his eyes with tears. The bastard actually had the balls to bring his family, his *child* into this. Agent Hahn liked to take risks, apparently.

"Do you want to make a difference, Silas?" The sincerity now in Hahn's voice, the compassion in the man's eyes, confused Kip. He hadn't been able to answer. So Kip laughed like it didn't matter, left the door open, and walked into the kitchen. "Beer?" he asked with more sarcasm than offer.

"No, thank you."

Kip shrugged and got a bottle from the cold box; then he turned and parked his beer and his hands on the counter. "What about whiskey?" The agent's cool demeanor got under his skin. Seeing Hahn standing there in his crisp suit and concerned gaze while Kip was drowning on the inside didn't go over very well. "No? How 'bout some polly-sue or ace?"

"How about a meal instead?"

Kip had shrugged. He was out of polly-sue anyway—the polypseudomorphine had knocked him out for a few days and then he'd used all the prescribed ace. . . . He hadn't eaten in . . . well, he couldn't remember how long. Just the thought of food made his stomach clench violently with need.

Before he knew it, he was seated in an eatery across the street from his apartment, not quite sure how he'd gotten there. He half listened to Hahn's proposal. Something about making a difference. Whatever.

They'd targeted him because of his engineering background and because now he had nothing left. Goddamn vultures. They were hoping he had a vendetta.

As much shit as Kip gave the man and his proposal, Hahn wasn't off point. He wanted someone to pay.

They'd talked about smugglers, about the postwar environment, about all the salvage and dangerous weapons drifting in space, just sitting on planets, in wreckage, waiting for the next terrorist to come along, recover it, and use it against innocent people.

When Hahn told him that ONI had a job for him, that they wanted him to crew on one of the most noted salvage crews who ran the Via Casilina, he'd nearly choked.

Agent Hahn was an excellent recruiter.

The more Kip considered it, the more the idea appealed to him.

Once back home and alone, he showered for the first time in . . . well, he couldn't remember exactly. And as the water washed him clean, he realized he wanted out. Off Sedra. And away from the void that now defined his life.

So he became an agent for the Office of Naval Intelligence.

They'd set him up with a new background, switched his name from Silas Kipley to Kip Silas—easier for him to remember than an entirely new name, they said (and given his mental state he was pretty sure they made the right call there). They gave him a new home, a new life, and eventually a new job, crewing on the *Ace of Spades*.

Who he once was no longer existed. That man was gone along with his family.

And now he was floating in space, wondering what the hell he had gotten himself into.

Rion Forge wasn't a terrorist. He'd figured that out pretty quickly, though he understood why ONI had placed him on the *Ace of Spades*. She was good at finding things, whether expensive or controversial. There was so much Covenant scrap scattered across the galaxy that it was impossible for ONI or the military to collect it all. So they kept their ears open and used civilians as much as their own considerable resources.

The heavy ordnance on the *Roman Blue* could have been used to kill innocents.

ONI had been right to put him here. He wanted them to find this stuff before anyone else did, before millions of other people died.

The cursor blinked at him from the small handheld pad ONI had issued. The scrambler was hidden in his quarters too. He had many gadgets that were a strange mix of human and alien. The tech was incredible, unlike anything Kip had seen. Niko might have found a tag, but it wasn't ONI's. Their tag remained hidden right where he'd placed it.

He was a traitor in their midst.

Kip had been invited and accepted into Rion's ragtag family. Just one look at the lounge and the living quarters and anyone could tell this wasn't some terrorist cell or fringe faction. *Ace of Spades* was a kick-ass ship, but she was also a well-loved home, decorated with mementos and objects found across the galaxy. And her crew was a tight band of oddball, risk-taking, adventure-seeking salvagers always out for a little danger and a good score.

And it gave Kip pause because the information he was sending back could get someone killed.

But then one or two was better than a million. . . .

A deep, conflicted sigh breezed past Kip's lips and he ran his hand down a scruffy cheek. Then he continued composing his message.

THIRTEEN

Ace of Spades, **approaching Arcadia**

"**W**ell, what do you think?"

Niko stood at the table across from Rion and eyed the buoy device. It was, for lack of a better description, the size of Cade's head, only rounder and not as sarcastic. Rion smiled at the thought.

Niko gnawed on his lip, then turned the hunk of metal this way and that, checking the casing and what little visible components there were.

"Well," he finally answered, "the good news is it's twenty-six years old, maybe more. UNSC stuff is hard to crack, but with this thing being technologically ancient, it shouldn't be an issue. I don't know the integrity of the chip inside or what kinds of encryption we'll come up against, but again, it's older tech and you're in the presence of a genius, so we'll probably get lucky. . . ."

Rion squeezed his shoulder. "Get started, then, genius. We'll stay parked on Arcadia's dark side until you figure it out. I'm going to check on Chalva."

It was a short walk back to the med bay. Before entering, she drew in a deep breath and tried to wipe the worry from her expression. She hadn't wanted to alarm the crew, but Ram's injuries were severe. At his bedside, she checked his monitors and then turned her attention to the man on the bed, wishing she could do more for him. Hell, that could be her lying there. Or Cade or Lessa. They'd all become targets.

With each wound she'd cleaned earlier, her hatred for the Sangheili grew. They had clearly tortured him. There was evidence of plasma burns and cuts so deep and dirty they'd turned angry and festering.

Still, the man struggled to hold on to consciousness. Even now, his eyelids were fluttering as though he knew she was there and was trying desperately to lift them.

"I need to put you in cryo," she told him gently. "We've done what we could, but you need a real doctor. . . ."

He blinked rapidly, his eyes bloodshot when they finally opened and found her. Despite the load of painkillers she'd given him, his breathing was pained and erratic. He was hurting, bad. Things were broken inside. And he required more help than she could give him. Cryo could buy him time—weeks, months even. . . .

He understood her words and nodded.

"We'll get you back to Venezia."

"Gek," he said, then took time and effort to swallow.

"Gek 'Lhar. Yeah. I know," she told him. "Don't worry, he'll get what's coming to him—I promise you that."

"I'm tagged." He grabbed her hand. "We're all tagged. Be . . . care—"

His grip went slack as he lost consciousness. Rion placed her hand on his chest, making a silent promise to set things right before calling Cade into the med bay to help transfer Ram to a cryo-chamber.

Niko worked for hours on the buoy, carefully taking it apart, the table strewn with tools. It was a slow process of dismantling one step at a time, and hoping the thing didn't have some sort of combustible tamper device.

Probably just loaded with encryptions.

That he could handle. Exploding things, not so much.

He'd seen enough violence on Aleria. Though, as glad as he was to be rid of that hot, dusty rock, without Aleria's courier guilds and their smuggling efforts, he never would have been introduced to the technology he'd grown to love. With the courier guild's slipspace-capable fleet of freighters, he'd been exposed at a young age to engines, support systems, FTL drives, and any bit of tech he could get his hands on and subsequently take apart . . . engines and FTL drives not included—he might have been young, but he didn't have a death wish. Mess with the couriers and you got your ass handed to you. And sometimes you got it handed to you without doing anything wrong. Just depended on the day.

There was a time when the courier guilds fought for all of Aleria. They'd risen against the might of the Mols'Desias mining union and justified violence on behalf of the population. Their smuggling had brought money and commerce and food into the markets and towns. But as time wore on and the guilds grew and split, it became less about the community and more about power.

Unlike Lessa, Niko hadn't been thrilled to leave it all behind. At first, he'd felt like he was just trading one gang for another. But it soon became apparent that Rion and Cade and Tesh—oh, how Niko missed giving that surly old engineer a hard time— were nothing like the guilders on Aleria. Tesh was simply too old to do any damage, though he made a lot of empty threats, and while Rion and Cade were definitely capable of raising hell, they saved that stuff for people who deserved it.

He genuinely liked Rion. He appreciated her blunt demeanor, dry humor, and ability to wield a blade. Honestly, she'd scared the shit out of him when she fought for him to be released from the guild. They didn't take kindly to would-be heroes coming in and saving their whipping boys and scapegoats.

It had happened so fast. A blur of him getting caught hacking her, her subsequent interrogation of him and Lessa . . . and when one of the couriers came upon them in the market, they'd had a little heart-to-heart on what was going to happen—namely, Rion taking them off world, courier guild be damned.

Needless to say, after it all went down, they left in a *big* hurry. Not that it mattered; they wouldn't be going back anytime soon.

Niko couldn't quite figure out Rion and Cade's deal, though. Sometimes on, sometimes off. And without the drama that one would expect from such an arrangement. But, hey, if it worked . . . Niko was learning real quick that things got lonely in space. Odd arrangements were the norm for travelers like him. Going into port was like a holiday every time. Of course, he went right to wherever the ladies hung out. Sometimes he got lucky, sometimes he struck out, and sometimes he simply made connections. There were a few girls he kept in touch with in New Tyne. . . .

The casing he was working on suddenly popped free. "Aha. Gotcha."

He resisted the urge to pull the guts from the buoy, instead looking for any small charges that might fry the chip. Rion would kill him if he screwed up now, after all the effort and risk that had gone into finding this thing in the first place.

His hands shook a little at the thought, sweat immediately beading his forehead. Why the hell did she always give him the hard jobs? It was like he was holding her heart in his hands. . . . "Yeah, no pressure," he muttered to himself, hoping the UNSC had opted out of self-destruct and had thought ahead to situations where the intel needed to be read quickly without the necessary codes being readily available in wartime scenarios.

Once he went through the insides, steady and careful, relief spread through him. And very soon, he found what he was after.

"Rion's heart, meet your liberator."

He retrieved the chip as though he were picking up and holding a newborn babe. Now all he had to do was break into the damn thing. Simple, right?

A few hours later, Niko was ready to pull his hair out.

At first, hearing the preprogrammed voice of "Serina" asking for security codes was cool. She sounded hot for an AI—all prim and proper like. He loved it.

For all of ten minutes.

Her repeated denials were starting to give him a complex. And a raging headache.

Bleary-eyed, Niko stared at the dark screen and input yet another decryption code, the sixth one he'd written. After that lengthy process was complete, he rested his forehead on his desk and waited.

He was nearly asleep when Serina's sultry reply, *"Access granted,"* sent him bolt upright.

It took a few seconds for his vision to come into focus,

but when it did he realized he hadn't been dreaming. "Access granted," he repeated tiredly, and then a jolt of reality hit him. "Access granted?!" He sat back, ran his fingers through his hair, and then linked them behind his head as the screen began filling up with precious code. "Serina, baby, I love you."

His heart was pounding, adrenaline giving him a final burst of energy. Enough to finish the job and copy the intel onto his drive before realizing he needed to hit the toilet, because his bladder was about to burst.

Rion was going to owe him big.

FOURTEEN

The deep pressure in Rion's chest built as she brought up the intel Niko had patched into her quarters. Absently, she rubbed the place above her sternum, the knotting sensation spreading and pushing all the way up her throat. The crew was anxious to know what the buoy contained, but she needed to read it alone first—a good idea given the fact that her insides were already in an uproar. She had no idea what she'd find, and she'd rather have a mental breakdown in the privacy of her own quarters.

Barely able to swallow, heart doing a wild dance, she pulled up the files, bypassing the long list of automatic systems reports and heading right for the priority alpha message.

Professor Anders captured. Obtained lock on her signal. Covenant ship leaving Arcadia, preparing

slipspace jump. Intercepted communication. . . . Hard
coordinates obtained. Spinning up FTL drives. Intend
to follow. Serina out.

Rion stared at the screen in utter disbelief. Coordinates. Actual coordinates. Not certain whether she was going to cheer or vomit, she shot to her feet and went straight for the whiskey. With a shaky hand, she splashed amber liquid into a glass and tipped the entire contents back. Refilled and repeated.

She swiped her hand across her mouth and let out a ragged breath, eyes stinging.

Coordinates. Dear God. She'd never thought . . .

Theories had abounded when the *Spirit of Fire* had been listed as MIA—and one in particular had caught her grandfather's interest. Several years after the ship went missing, a rumor began floating around that she might have been involved in a battle at Arcadia. No real proof or intel, though.

But now, Captain Webb's journal and the buoy confirmed that rumor as truth.

They'd been alive when they went after Anders. And if Rion's memory was correct, nothing ever came around the rumor mill of any sightings after that.

Until now.

With a shaky hand, she keyed the coordinates into the ship's nav system to pull up a star map. Only no shipping maps or old military maps in *Ace*'s databanks appeared. The coordinates were outside of any mapped system they had at their disposal. "Uncharted space," she murmured, sitting back and sighing heavily.

The whiskey had warmed her belly and had taken off the volatile edge she'd felt earlier. *Uncharted space.* They'd be flying in blind. No idea what they'd find or what they might run into, though it was relatively safe to assume the Covenant ship had known where it was going. It would hardly run itself into a sun or planet.

Though that was twenty-six years ago. . . .

Rion stared at the coordinates for another few minutes before alerting the crew. They were about to go sailing in unknown waters.

"Uh, Cap?"

"Yeah, Less?"

"We have a ship approaching Arcadia. It's the Covenant war-freighter."

Looked like Gek had finally found them. Time to go where he couldn't follow. Rion leaned forward. "Sending you coordinates. Let's get the hell out of here."

PART FOUR

SNAKE EYES

FIFTEEN

Ace of Spades, uncharted space, four days later

Ace dropped out of slipspace and traveled another four and a half hours at top sub-light-speed before finally approaching the coordinates given by the *Spirit of Fire*'s AI, Serina.

Visually, there seemed to be nothing out there in the way of scrap—just darkness broken up by the distant flecks of other stars and systems.

From her chair on the bridge, Rion checked the data again. "Cade?"

"I'm seeing what you're seeing, but this is it."

Rion's finger tapped on the armrest, quickly and tersely, a tiny reflection of the enormous tension and impatience stirring inside her. "Take a look around. You all know the drill. Let's treat this like we usually do. Start hunting. When you find something, let me know." She stood and headed off the bridge.

"Cap," Lessa called her back, "I'm picking up a small dwarf signature about three points on the starboard quarter. It's the only thing in range. . . ."

Rion returned to main controls. Cade and Niko were monitoring as well. "Guys?" she asked them.

Cade shook his head. "Still nothing."

"Same here. Just the dwarf," Niko added.

"All right, take us to the star, then, and we'll see what we can find. Less, how long?"

Lessa input and received her calculations. "Um, an hour and thirty minutes if we do a two-G burst and coast?" Unsure, she looked to Cade.

Amusement flickered across his face. "That's about right, give or take."

"Good. Make it happen. Let me know when we get there." Rion left the bridge.

Without bothering to change into workout gear, she went to the small gym attached to the med bay, first stopping by to check Ram's cryo-chamber before stepping onto the treadmill and walking—walking and thinking, the kind of vague, unfocused mind-rambling that meant nothing and led nowhere.

An hour and change later, Cade called her back.

When Rion arrived on deck, instead of black space greeting her, the viewscreen was filled with a field of asteroids orbiting a brown dwarf star.

"Move us in for a closer look." Rion stepped to her chair, standing behind it, hands gripping the backrest. All the calm she'd found on the treadmill completely evaporated, replaced with a hum of anticipation as Cade navigated *Ace* toward the asteroid belt.

"Holy shit. Is that . . ." Niko popped out of his chair and leaned over his controls, peering in disbelief. "Is that . . . *metal*?"

Rion approached the viewscreen with a frown on her face and butterflies in her gut. He was right. Massive chunks of alloy floated by amid smaller bits and pieces of what appeared to be wreckage and infrastructure on a massive scale. Conduits, cables, masonry . . . Part of a bridge sailed past, its great pylon still sunk into a large chunk of rock. The scale of it, the entire scene, was surreal and unexpected.

"Uh . . ." Lessa said. "Someone tell me that's not a mountain."

Except, as crazy as it seemed, there *was* a mountain out there, floating past them as though a colossal hand had reached down through the clouds of some forgotten planet, sunk its enormous fingers into the ground, and ripped the jagged peak from its range and flung it into space.

Cade shot to his feet. "Wait. That's a ship fragment."

Rion saw it too: the sleek piece of metal slowly tumbling into view. "Niko, can you magnify that?" In seconds, an image of what appeared to be a wing came into focus, though unlike any that Rion had ever seen. "Grab the image and move it to the table." She stepped to his console, leaned over it, and hit a button on the commpad. "Hey, Kip, we need you up here."

A beat passed. "Sure. Be right up."

As they waited, the mood on the bridge was one of shock, excitement, and confusion. Cade was the first to say what they all were thinking. "This is planetary debris."

"Could it be what's left of the coordinates?" Lessa asked as Kip came onto the bridge. "The coordinates the *Spirit of Fire* was headed to? Maybe there was a battle and the whole planet was somehow destroyed, and some of it came here, getting pulled into the star's orbit."

Kip joined Rion at the table as the others discussed the possibilities. "What do you think?" she asked him as he paused by her side, his attention already glued on the wing.

"Boss, you're not going to believe this," Niko said.

She was almost afraid to ask. "What is it?"

"Getting a strange . . . hold on." He frowned. "This keeps getting weirder and weirder. There's some kind of energy shield out there. . . ."

Rion hurried to Niko's console. "Where?" she asked, peering over his shoulder.

"There." He pointed at the blip on his screen. "It's in the debris field."

"Cade, navigate us into the field and put us within visual range of that signal," Rion ordered.

She straightened and watched with rapt attention as *Ace* eased into the field, Cade executing a series of thrusts and drifts in order to maneuver safely amid the debris and on through to the coordinates of the energy signature.

"What is *that*?" Niko asked as *Ace* reversed thrust and then settled in orbit with a large chunk of detritus ringed by a shield of translucent blue. Beyond the shield was a ruin built on a jagged, broken bit of earth the size of a large freighter and blackened as though flash-burned.

"I've never seen a wing design like this before," Kip said under his breath, still studying the image.

"Niko?" Rion prompted, more interested in the ruins.

"The shield is reading similar to Covenant energy barriers. But . . . not." He glanced up at her. "But where there's a shield, there's a reason. Right?"

"There's an atmosphere down there, and gravity," Lessa said. "The levels are near perfect for us. You think this might be human? A colony? Or what's left of one?"

No one said it, but they were all thinking about the *Spirit of Fire* and her crew of eleven thousand souls. . . .

Rion refused to get her hopes up, but that barrier had to be protecting *something*. And if there were humans down there, if that chunk was some sort of refuge, they were honor-bound to take a look. She went to her chair and sat down, thoughts churning, adrenaline pumping, and her good sense warring with the desire to throw caution to the wind and surge ahead. The crew glanced back at her, ready for orders, just as eager as she was to move forward. "We proceed with caution. Let's test that barrier."

It took some time for Niko to tinker with his beloved drone, Michelle—another one of his modified toys—before they were able to launch her into space and navigate her toward the energy barrier.

"She's entering now." Niko's nose was glued to his controls as Michelle slipped through the barrier. A few seconds passed before reports began flowing in. "She looks good. . . . Ooh, this is . . . surprising. Picking up life signs. Signal is faint, though, coming from the interior, possibly several meters down from the surface." His head lifted and he met Rion's gaze. "Everything else looks golden. Michelle says we're good to go in."

"Double-check everything." Rion pulled up the readouts on her small screen, scanning them, looking for any sign that might indicate caution. But Michelle's integrity remained the same— her sensors indicated green across the board. From all accounts, the energy barrier was a simple environmental field, preventing gases from entering or escaping, and allowing solid matter to pass through unharmed.

"No, there's nothing," Niko said. "All reports say we're good."

Cade was currently monitoring *Ace*'s position in the field while Lessa kept an eye on rogue debris in their vicinity. Kip was still examining the wing, turning the image this way and that and then keying in searches, trying to find a match. She hadn't had much time to look at it, but as Kip continued his examination, something stirred in her memory and—

"*Rion*." Cade's voice drew her attention away from the wing.

The crew was staring at her, waiting as *Ace* was poised at the edge of the energy shield. "Take us in."

Ace slipped through the shield. The strange translucent glow rolled over the bow and continued on through the ship like a blue-tinted wave, covering everything in its path. Rion half expected it to tingle or burn—or worse—as it traveled over them, but there was nothing. She checked her sensors once they were inside the shield and all systems remained normal.

"Niko, switch to ground view." Rion watched the viewscreen as the surface appeared. There were signs of vegetation, long dead, and a wide flagstone road that led to the building, though it was cracked and buckled in places. Because of the deterioration and the state of the road and structure, it was difficult to match a civilization to the ruins they were seeing. They had to take a closer look.

First, they needed to find a good spot to land *Ace*. Cade, however, was already one step ahead and guiding the ship toward part of a large slab of uneven rock that rose from the ground, part of a cliff face where *Ace* might find a measure of protection.

SIXTEEN

Unknown ruin, debris field, uncharted space

After a quick rundown with the crew, Rion and Cade suited up and paid a visit to the weapons store. One assault rifle, three sidearms, and a sack of grenades later, they were out of the air lock and heading down the ramp. The surface wasn't entirely dark; the energy barrier cast a soft blue haze over the ground, reminding Rion of a moonlit night back on Earth.

"Confirming earlier readings. Pressure is right on target. Temp's a balmy sixty-one degrees." Cade moved slowly over the ground while scanning the readouts on his commpad. "Nitrogen, oxygen, argon, carbon dioxide . . . Gravity's almost on target too, a little under one G." With that, he released the locks on his helmet.

"Cade—"

Helmet off, he breathed in deeply and gave her a megawatt smile. "Atmosphere. Check."

"Smart-ass." Rion removed her helmet, clipping it to the back of her waistband before pressing the nodule on her collar. "Switching to wrist comms and external audio."

"The life signs are still too faint for a clean reading. Definitely underground, though. We'll keep monitoring and let you know if anything changes," Lessa said, her voice loud and clear through Rion's earpiece.

"Michelle's at the end of that road. There's a door into the structure," Niko added. "Forty degrees from your position. Should be about sixty meters or so."

"So you mean right around the corner," Cade replied in a flat tone, shaking his head.

"Well, if you want to get technical."

Rion smiled. "Ready?"

Cade answered by pulling his assault rifle from his back and over his shoulder. "Am now."

They kept to the rocks, mirroring the path of the flagstone road and keeping their eyes peeled for any movement and checking the motion sensors in their comms, which were able to pick up movement within a ten-meter radius. Not exactly top-of-the-line sensor grade, but useful nonetheless.

"Any luck on that wing, Kip?" Rion asked as they edged around several blocks of cut stone.

Kip's tone sounded a little bewildered. "Uh. Yeah. Some of the designs match up to a couple of images I found from a xeno-archaeological paper. That wing, I think, is—"

"Forerunner," Rion whispered as they came around the stones to find the door Niko had mentioned. Where the blackened surface of the structure gave way to smooth stone, a line of Forerunner glyphs was visible. Ancient. Precise. And utterly impressive. "This entire place is a Forerunner site," she said with disbelief, turning in a circle and now seeing the ruins for what they were.

"Any movement on those life signs?" Cade asked as they proceeded to the threshold of the tall entryway.

"The building must have multiple floors underground," Niko replied. "Whoever or whatever it is must be way down. Hard to tell how many—getting a lot of strange signal interference."

"If this is Forerunner," Cade said, pausing to glance at Rion, "then who the hell is down there?"

"Good question. Let's find out."

Rion slipped inside the building. A few steps in, a blue beam swept over her and Cade. Immediately after, the floor lit up with a bluish light filling in glyphs and patterns in the floor and forming a path that led them inside to a center console that glowed more brightly than anything in the area.

"Must've tripped a sensor," Cade said from behind her.

The room was smaller than she imagined, a circular space with a massive central column and two corridors leading off into darkness on either side. But it was the console that drew her. It was clearly made for a being taller than the average human. The display contained more strange symbols and shapes, pulsing blue and oddly hypnotizing.

Her attention snagged on a domed pad with the outline of what looked like a hand. Her fingers twitched. She reached up.

Cade grabbed her wrist. "What are you doing?"

His grip was firm and unyielding. For just the briefest of moments, she wanted to fight him, to jerk her arm away and slap her hand on that pad. "I don't know." What *was* she doing? The sensation passed, leaving her curious and a little shaken. She searched Cade's face, trying to ascertain if he was similarly affected. "You don't want to touch it?"

His mouth twitched and he gave her the drollest look she'd ever seen.

There were a million ways he could have responded. And she had to give the man credit, because he said none of them. Though his eyes crinkled good-naturedly at the corners and his grin was blinding.

Rion tried to suppress her smile. Cade could tease and flirt with the best of them. But he was never crude, never showed her disrespect in front of the crew. And that went a long way in her estimation. Warmth spread through her, and there were those possibilities again, rising up fresh and hopeful. . . .

Not the time. Later, though. Maybe later.

With a shake of her head, she tabled the humor and distraction, turning back to the room, noting the two passageways on the left and right of the central column. The walls weren't lit, but the floor leading down the passages glowed with glyphs.

"Right or left?" she asked.

"Guys, get out of there!" Niko shouted. "Get out of there now! Shit! There's a ship. It's been inside the barrier this whole time. Behind the ruins. Must have been in stealth. . . . It's powering up."

"It's a Covenant war-freighter," Kip said in a clipped voice. "Same sig as the one on Laconia."

Anger rose hot inside her. Damn it. "We were tagged," she replied, Ram Chalva's warning ringing in her head. Gek 'Lhar had followed them to the debris field. And while they took their sweet time being cautious, she'd inadvertently given the Sangheili a two-hour advantage to settle in and get to the goods before she did.

And now they were about to be ambushed.

"What should we do?" Lessa's panic threaded through each word. "Take off? What? What do you want me to do?"

"Have they locked on?"

"Uh . . . no. But they had to have seen us. *Wait! It's locking on! It's locking on!*"

"Get that ramp up, engage shields, and fly," Rion instructed in a firm tone. "Use the debris field as cover."

Cade was ahead of her as they ran for the door. "Go now, Less," he ordered. "I'll lay down cover." He cleared the building. "War-freighter is up and over the back side of the ruins. I've got them in sight."

"Life sign on your six!" Niko shouted as Rion was suddenly grabbed from behind, lifted off her feet, and thrown back into the room. Shock stole her breath as she went airborne and then slammed into the central console.

Pain exploded through her back. Whiplash wrenched her neck. *Dear God.* Her vision went fuzzy and her stomach turned as she tried to rise. Her hands flattened on the console in an attempt to push off. The entire panel flared to life, blue illuminating every pattern and glyph.

With a groan Rion slid off the console and hit the floor.

The *stomp, stomp, stomp* of armored feet on flagstone echoed in the space like thunder. She lifted her head and saw the air warble before a two-and-a-half-meter tall Sangheili appeared out of thin air. Stealth tech. No wonder he'd caught them all off guard.

This had to be Gek 'Lhar. It was the same hinge-head she'd seen through her binoculars on Laconia. His shoulders were hunched, his bare arms thick and long, hands clenching and unclenching as though he was already squeezing the life out of her.

Warnings fired through her brain, some primitive part urging for flight, not fight. Rion ignored the hot, aching flares throughout her back and neck, and straightened to edge around the console. Escape lay between her and the alien. Moving slowly toward one of the dark passageways, she tried to angle toward the exit, hoping he'd track her movement and turn enough so that she could listen to that urge to run and hopefully slip past him.

Against an eight-foot-tall, three-hundred-plus-pound former Covenant commander, running was definitely her best option.

Rion's comm erupted with the crews' shouts and Cade's orders. A loud explosion echoed from beyond the walls and shook the ground. She knew that sound—Cade had tossed a frag grenade or two, providing distraction and cover for *Ace*. The debris field was a good place to play hide-and-seek. Lessa had become a damn good pilot. And with Niko and Kip providing support, they'd be fine.

Rion, on the other hand . . .

As Gek moved, a bright flash on his shoulder harness caught her eye. Oh hell. Were those *dog tags*? Fear slid cold and icy beneath her skin. She pulled her sidearm from her holster and the Sangheili warrior threw back his head, his four mandibles spreading wide, and issued what sounded like laughter, the sound guttural and deep and full of confidence. His disdain for an insignificant human female and her weapon shone in his amused gray eyes with a ferocious glee.

"Well shit," Rion muttered.

And then he moved another step, allowing her to see what hovered behind him. And that sure as hell changed things.

It was a luminary. He'd found the luminary either on the *Radiant Perception*. Or here in the ruins.

Damn it.

Fear took a momentary backseat to her salvager's heart. She wanted it. Rion straightened her aching back and drew upon all the bravado she had left, no matter how false, and tilted her head. "Been looking for one of those."

The Sangheili's eyes narrowed to ghostly slits. His sonorous voice rang out in response. "Translate," Rion said quietly. There was a three-second delay as her earpiece played a computer-generated voice.

"How dare you defile the sanctuary of the gods! How dare you stand upon their foundations and look with unclean longing at their gifts! I shall find honor in ridding this holy structure of your human stench."

He bleeds just like anything else, she told herself. Repeatedly.

The console's light grew brighter. A disembodied voice suddenly filled the room, seeming to come from everywhere all at once. *"Reclaimer?"* Static stole the words that came next, but they were excited words, jubilant, and relieved. *"You came, Reclaimer. Thank goodness you're here!"*

Gek 'Lhar glared at the console, the voice appearing to make him awed and furious at the same time. He leveled a deadly glare her way as though she had something to do with it. But then she supposed she had—she'd touched that damn hand scanner when the hinge-head had tossed her into the console.

She shrugged. "Your fault, big guy. Not mine."

His energy sword activated with a bright flash and a *whoosh*.

Rion raised her M6 and fired at his unprotected head. Incredibly quick, he was already ducking to the right. One shot pinged off his chest harness, the other sailed just over his skull. Outside, Cade was still actively engaged. She had no idea how many ships and companions the Sangheili had with him or what her own crew was dealing with outside the walls.

"Unclean vermin," he growled as he moved toward her with surprising speed, drawing up short as two other Sangheili

appeared from the dark passageway. *"Go, brothers,"* he ordered them. *"This will not take long."* They ran for the door.

Shit. Cade was just outside. "Cade, you have incoming behind you! Lessa, swing around and provide support for Cade. And take out that war-freighter already, will you?"

An explosion lit the entrance.

"No worries, Less, I got 'em," Cade said, breathing heavily. "Nothing like thermite in your face, eh, boys? I'm running low on surprises and options here. *Ace*, how you guys doing up there?"

Niko's whoop came through the comms. "Now I know why you love this ship!"

"We're picking up four in the war-freighter and three on the ground," Kip said.

"Make that one left on the ground," Cade said. "I'm on my way, Forge."

It only took Rion a half second to realize—

Gek 'Lhar's back was to the entrance now, his energy sword casting an eerie glow. Cade was running in blind.

"No, wait! Cade! Don't—" she shouted, surging forward in a desperate attempt.

But Cade was already inside. And Gek was already turning. Cade saw what was going to happen and couldn't stop it. With a split-second moment of clarity and ingenuity, he slid the bag of grenades across the floor toward Rion as the energy sword plunged effortlessly through his chest.

With a scream of horror, Rion ran, leapt on a console, and from there jumped on the Sangheili's back. She stuck the muzzle of her M6 against his skull and fired at the same moment he struck her on the side of her head with his forearm. The bullet sliced across his left eye and ricocheted off his chest armor. Gek roared as blood spilled from the wound. He reached up with both hands, grabbed Rion by the shoulders, and slung her over his head.

She hit the wall and felt a stinging snap in her lower back.

Nausea and pain rolled through her, one sickening wave after another. But she pushed on, shocked and horrified, crawling over to the bag of grenades. Inside, nothing but a flashbang and a frag. A frag would kill them all. And a flashbang wouldn't accomplish much because she didn't intend to cause a distraction and run. She wasn't leaving Cade.

Panting heavily, she gritted her teeth and forced herself to stand, unable to stop the groan of hurt that tore from her throat. A cold sweat covered her skin. Her vision wavered. The pain shooting down her legs was unbearable.

The Sangheili leaned over and ripped Cade's dog tags from his neck. Then he canted slightly in her direction, thick indigo blood running down the left side of his face as he bared his nasty, pointed, blood-covered teeth, his jaws vibrating. The hate in that one good eye burned hot and sparked inside her a cold, deadened rage.

She lifted the grenade.

The disembodied voice stopped its incessant chattering to say, *"An explosion of that magnitude would . . ."*

Rion ignored it completely. She knew exactly what the frag would do.

And so did Gek 'Lhar.

There was no mercy left inside her, no sense of self-preservation, no fear—just a dazzling need for retribution. It built inside, bristling and biting. Her eyes stung hot with unshed tears, but she never looked away, never gave the murderous creature the satisfaction. She wanted him to see the lengths to which she was willing to go.

She lifted the grenade higher and flicked the safety.

They stared at each other for a long, tense moment. She'd do it. If he took one goddamn step—

He glanced at the luminary, his hesitation clear. He wanted the fight, but that device—to him, a sacred relic—was more important than running the risk of damage. To him, it was more important than anything else. With an evil glint in his one good eye, he hooked Cade's dog tags on his shoulder to hang with the others, sneered at her, then stepped over Cade's body and maneuvered the luminary out the door.

Rion heard the crew's voices in her comm, but they were just background noise now.

Everything was background noise. Everything but Cade.

SEVENTEEN

Forerunner ruin, debris field, uncharted space

The pain in Rion's back rolled over her in nasty waves. Bile rose in her throat as she sank to her knees and crawled to Cade's side. His hands were on his chest, the massive wound having been cauterized by the effects of the plasma sword. His breath was shallow, coming in small, faint wisps. His eyes were dazed, unfocused and blinking, as though he were trying desperately to stay lucid with every blink.

"Cade." Her voice broke as he turned his head. His hand flailed, searching for her. She grabbed it and held tight. Quickly, she examined the gaping wound, wanting to do something, to ease his pain, to fix it.

But it was too late. There was nothing she could do.

He squeezed and her attention returned to his pale face. Emotion swam among tears as he stared at her with a vague smile. He went to speak, but blood bubbled up, choking him instead. His throat worked, trying to swallow it down.

"Shh. You don't have to—"

"It's okay, Forge," he forced out. "Guess it . . . wasn't so easy after all."

His eyelids fluttered. Rion's hand tightened and she leaned over him. "Cade, no," she cried, cheek to cheek, tears falling hot from her eyes.

"It's okay," he barely whispered.

She lifted her head. His eyes were closed now. His shaking ceased. His body went quiet.

"Niko," Rion managed, as raw fury lit a path through every nerve in her body. "Unload everything we have on that ship."

"Way ahead of you, boss," he said, his voice angry and broken.

The crew's communications faded into the background. Rion registered it all, a small part of her keeping track as *Ace* pursued the Covenant war-freighter after it had swept in to pick up Gek 'Lhar and the subsequent chase through the debris field.

If there was any chance to stop that ship, they had to do it without her.

Which was just as well. She wasn't leaving Cade.

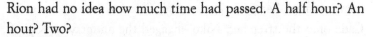

Rion had no idea how much time had passed. A half hour? An hour? Two?

Whatever. It felt like a lifetime either way.

Gek and his crew had made their way through the debris field and fled the system.

Lessa, Niko, and Kip came at some point with a grav stretcher from the med bay. She stared at it, its presence bringing up the stark reality that she couldn't remain there forever, couldn't sit with Cade as long as she wanted. And soon she'd have to say good-bye. But this good-bye . . . oh, this one would be so very hard.

Tears stung her eyes again, but she forced them down along with the lump in her throat.

Lessa knelt by Cade's side, her nose and eyes red from crying. Niko sank down beside his sister and put his arm around her. His eyes were rimmed with tears, old streaks dried on his young face.

They mourned for Cade. It had never occurred to them that someone might die—or maybe it had, but the idea had been just a faint shadow, a whisper, nothing more.

Watching them grieve was another kind of pain Rion couldn't have prepared for. It wasn't supposed to end like this; her personal demons and her search for answers weren't supposed to get anyone killed.

"Did you bring pain inhibitors?" she asked Kip. He was quiet, head down. She couldn't see his face as he prepared the stretcher.

He glanced over his shoulder, eyes haunted and nodded, then rooted around in the bag sitting on the stretcher. He knelt next to her to administer the medication, but she took the syringe from him. "I'll do it. Just see to Cade."

And then she injected the medication into her thigh, closing her eyes and counting down the seconds for the drug to flow and begin to mask her pain, just enough time for the crew to move Cade onto the stretcher. Niko engaged the antigravity. Kip offered her a hand, and the kindness was more than she could take as the inhibitor washed over her, unlocking the tenuous control she had over her emotions. Guilt flowed in like a tsunami. And as she stared up at Kip and his outstretched hand, she felt weak for the first time in a long while.

There was something in his eyes, a kind of understanding and a depth she hadn't seen before . . . as though he understood pain and grief on a deep and very personal level.

He gestured once more, telling her to accept his help. And eventually, she did.

"Wait! Where are you going?"

They all paused at the disembodied sound, the sheer desperation clear in the high-pitched tone. Rion had completely forgotten about the strange voice; it had gone silent when Cade died.

"If you must go, take me with you. I am here to assist, Reclaimers."

In a semidrugged daze, Rion blew out a weary breath and told the crew to take Cade back to the ship.

She watched them leave, and a bleak, withering darkness worked its way inside her, taking root, encompassing her emotions within a hard, bitter shell. Her grief must be contained because she couldn't fall apart now or leave her ship and crew without a leader, without strength to lean on, or a sharp mind to get them home.

She failed Cade. God, how she failed.

But it wouldn't, *couldn't* happen again.

Her steps were slow and measured as she made her way to the console. Even with the meds, her back burned with harsh, unrelenting pain. She wiped the back of her forearm across her wet face, then rested both hands on the console and forced words from her exhausted body. "All right, whatever you are. You have five minutes."

"I am," the voice began with pomp, and then stalled as though forgetting its identity. *"I am . . . the caretaker of this facility. I am . . . You have returned. No. Different. Ah. Yes. Reclaimer. I am here. Trapped in this console. This chip. Just a little bit. I am a bit. I'm a little bit . . . leftover."*

"You're a Forerunner AI."

"Perhaps, yes? But alas, just a little bit." It let out a strange metallic-sounding sigh. *"Fragmented. Name and designation lost. Little bit. Just a little bit left. Kept running, kept jumping, kept copying . . . Piece to piece. Bit to bit. You are a Reclaimer. Not all is lost."*

"A Reclaimer?"

"Of course. I have held in trust all of it, the whole . . . The whole . . . The entire . . ."

"The entire what? The entire planet? Is that what you mean?"

"No, not a planet. Not really. But yes, I think. Have you come for the ships?"

She thought of the wing they'd seen in the debris field. "You mean Forerunner ships?"

"All right. Yes. They are all around us, bits and pieces. I'm sorry. I could not stop them. I had to jump. Kept jumping, kept copying, piece to piece . . . But wait. I remember. You did this."

At the change of his voice, Rion tensed. "Did what exactly?"

"Destroyed. You destroyed. All of it."

"No. We just arrived. We didn't destroy anything."

"But I saw you. I saw your Reclaimer ship. Shield at fifteen percent. We should go. I must serve."

"What ship?"

"UNSC designated CFV-88 Phoenix-class colony ship, Spirit of Fire, *of course. I seem to have misplaced some data. . . . The copies, you see. So many copies. But this is remembered, this is the last thing. Last things are always remembered."*

Traces of the absurd snaked through her drug-dulled mind. Laughter bubbled up, the dazed and ridiculous kind that came because she couldn't process anything else. She'd reached her limit.

She'd come looking for that very ship, had followed a trail from the *Roman Blue*, to the *Radiant Perception*, to the buoy, and now here to a Forerunner AI that couldn't remember its name . . . but it *could* remember the ship that had destroyed its world.

She'd achieved so much in such a short amount of time, and yet she felt further away from her goals than ever. And did those goals even matter now?

"I'm not certain this qualifies as humorous. Humor is defined as a mood or state of mind wherein one feels or expresses joy, elation, mirth, hilarity—"

"I know what humor is."

"You are a Reclaimer. It is my duty. My duty to wait on you. Or is it wait for you? I simply cannot tell the difference. Can you?"

"Not really." Rion wiped the tears from her eyes. "So you want off this rock?"

"Yes."

"Fine," she said tiredly. "Why the hell not."

"One moment, please."

The console's light began to recede from the display and merge with the center dome. The dome slid back, revealing a chip with similar etchings as those on the console.

"You may remove me now."

EIGHTEEN

Ace of Spades, debris field, uncharted space

As soon as she was on board, Rion engaged the air lock and shuffled slowly up the stairs and down the narrow walk to the med bay, her inhibitor wearing thin. The crew would have used the service elevator to take Cade's body to the bay, and that bleak image filled her mind without mercy.

Lessa was alone in the med bay, standing vigil, looking scared and stricken and so damn young, her arms hugging herself, unsure of what to do next.

She glanced up and Rion's heart gave a painful squeeze at the wide-eyed grief in the young woman's eyes. "What do we do?" Lessa asked, her lips wet with tears. "I don't know what to do."

Rion didn't want to see anyone, nor did she feel like talking or comforting. And yet, that's exactly what she did. Lessa grabbed tightly on to her and cried and shook. Her wild, curly hair itched

Rion's chin and smelled of sweat and old fear, a reminder of how frantic the girl must have been, flying solo, engaging a Covenant war-freighter.

"Hey. You did great today. You took care of *Ace*."

Lessa lifted her head slightly and stared over Rion's shoulder at Cade's body. "But not him. I didn't take care of him."

"You didn't have to. That was my job."

"You did the best you could. We all did, right?"

Tightness spread across Rion's chest and she attempted a smile. "I'll see to him. Go get some rest, check on your brother. . . ."

Rion waited until Lessa left the bay, then limped to the med cabinet and rooted inside for another shot of pain inhibitor. After the needle went in, she stayed bowed for a while before straightening and facing the stretcher. The only times she'd had to tend the dead in the past was when she helped Unn prepare Birger, and then again when Unn had died. She knew what to do. She'd just never thought she'd be doing it for one of her crew, much less Cade.

She went slowly: the time and focus on removing Cade's gear, cleaning him, and then retrieving his dress blues from his quarters was a ritual she desperately needed. This was her farewell. She didn't speak a word, didn't shed a tear, didn't think of anything else but each small movement, each simple task, each tiny button.

She'd loved him. And they'd been so damn stupid, so afraid of losing each other, that they'd kept their hearts distant and out of their relationship as much as they could. And now he was gone, leaving a deep well of regret.

Two and a half hours later, he was ready.

Breaking the solitude was difficult, but she hit the ship-wide comm. "Less, take us to the dwarf star." She didn't need to say why or issue any other instructions. They'd know.

Once *Ace* was under way, Rion went to her quarters, stripped down, and stepped into the shower. When the first drops of water hit her skin, she stopped holding it all in. Guilt and regret were terrible weights, but she took them as her own, bore them hard on her shoulders, sinking to her knees, the water stinging and painful against her bruised back as she sobbed.

"He's with his family now." Hope and worry clung to Lessa's quiet statement. "He's got to be, right? There has to be more out there. . . ." She glanced at Rion, then watched the personnel pod shoot into space on a trajectory aimed straight into the heart of the dwarf star. "Right?"

Rion swallowed the lump in her throat. She thought of those she'd lost: her grandfather, her Aunt Jillian, the Birgers. . . . Dear God, she hoped there was more. Lacking a staunch religious belief, all she could do was hope. "Yeah . . . I think he's finally home."

She turned for her chair and out of habit was about to issue flight orders to Cade.

Her eyes stung, but she stowed the grief. *Just get everyone home. Then you can fall apart.* "Kip, spin up the FTL. We're getting out of here."

With one last look at the pod, just a speck now against the backdrop of the star, Rion settled in and prepared to jump.

"Uh, Cap?" Kip said, frowning at his display. "We're spinning up too fast. I don't know what's—"

A familiar disembodied voice filtered through the bridge. *"Apologies. That would be me, engineer."*

Stunned, Rion began checking systems. "You're a chip, sitting on my desk in my quarters," she said calmly. The thing shouldn't be talking to them; she hadn't inserted the chip into any of *Ace's* networks.

"Most of me is, yes. But when you touched the pad on my console, I was able to ride a directed energy beam into your forearm unit. And now I've linked to your main data systems. I have been assessing your systems and technologies, which were severely in need of service. This ship lacks any moderately intelligent construct and your slipspace capabilities were positively ancient—"

"Were?"

"Oh, yes. I have made several adjustments to your drives and systems. Particularly your navigational systems, mapping systems, communications systems, and your slipspace drives. You will see an increase in speed and precision. If you will but lend me your engineer to make physical modifications, I can increase that by orders of magnitude . . . ."

"Whoa, whoa, whoa." Niko was halfway out of his chair. "This is an AI?"

"Yes. I am . . . A little bit. Just a little bit."

"And you've been messing with my comms?"

"Messing . . . I do not understand this. One moment. Ah. Yes. Messing. Yes. I have indeed 'messed' with your comms. I am also able to streamline your energy output and stealth capabilities and rework your baffling engines to be more productive."

Rion had just been hanging on, maintaining her balance. And now a Forerunner AI had invaded her ship. She was tempted to put her head in her hands and give in to the weary, grief-stricken laughter that pushed at her chest. But she did neither of those things, because as surreal as the moment was, as unexpected and potentially disastrous, there was a very clear silver lining.

Considering this silver lining was like teetering on the edge of a cliff, pretty sure you *might* be able to fly.

"Is this a wise course of action, Cap?" Kip asked, taking her silence as acceptance of the AI's invasion.

"Of course it is wise. My purpose is to assist and monitor. I do not deviate. I cannot deviate. I do not infiltrate; I serve."

Offended, Niko opened his mouth to argue that point. Infiltrate was exactly what the AI had done, but Rion shook her head, telling him to stand down.

The engines grew louder as *Ace*'s FTL spun. They were preparing to enter slipspace at near light-speed. And Rion felt like she was about to fall, because she knew once the words were out of her mouth, there was no going back and everything was going to change. Again.

A cold resolution settled in, hard and necessary. She did, in fact, have goals. She wanted revenge for Cade. She wanted answers. She wanted someone else to hurt for a change, to pay. . . .

Her father was still out there. And she wanted a goddamn happy ending.

She wanted to *win*.

The AI, even in its fragmented state, could help her do that.

"Do it."

"Excellent. I shall start immediately. Entering slipspace now . . . Captain Forge."

Ahead, a portal ate a hole in space, widening . . . growing larger, brighter. The flash as they entered was blinding, the stars stretching for the briefest of moments, bleeding into nothing but darkness.

"We shall arrive at Venezia in sixty of your Earth minutes."

"Right," Niko said in disbelief. "I'll believe it when I see it."

A fog seemed to fall over Rion. And the crew wasn't faring

any better. They were exhausted and edgy. Shadows lurked under Niko's red eyes. Rion had worked him hard over the last few weeks, and now he had such tragedy to deal with. And Lessa— her usual happy demeanor was gone and she seemed fragile and worn. Kip kept to himself; Rion had no idea how he fared, but every time their eyes met she saw hurt and regret.

"Everyone take some time," she told them.

"What about you?" Niko looked over his shoulder.

A ghost of a smile thinned her lips. "I'll make sure our new AI is right and we get back to Venezia in one piece."

"Of course I'm right. And not just a little bit. My calculations are correct. There would be no reason to—"

"Little Bit?" Rion cut in, pinching the bridge of her nose.

"Yes, Captain Forge?"

"Have you taken a look at our environmental systems?"

"Of course. I have modified the systems. . . ."

She rubbed her eyes as "Little Bit" kept speaking and realized that trying to find something for a highly advanced ancient AI to do was just about pointless.

". . . and once my chip has been inserted, I will be able to increase my presence. . . ."

NINETEEN

Ace of Spades, 25,000 kilometers above Venezia, Qab system

Rion stood at the observation window in *Ace*'s lounge and stared at Venezia from twenty-five thousand kilometers.

They had indeed arrived in sixty minutes.

The full realization of what the fragmented construct had been able to accomplish was astounding. And frightening. She had a Forerunner artificial intelligence in her possession, something that most interested parties would kill for.

And in turn, the AI had in its possession firsthand information about the *Spirit of Fire*.

As exciting as that should have been, it came in a package wrapped in gray and shadowed by death.

Lessa's voice came over the comm. "Captain?"

"Go ahead."

"Kathy from Venezia TC is asking if we want to secure our

usual berth? It's available. Or you just want to hang in orbit for a while?"

"Secure the berth and request immediate medical assistance for Ram."

As *Ace* received permission to enter the planet's airspace, Rion went to the bridge, relieved Lessa, and flew the ship in herself. Once they were docked, she released the air locks and opened the cargo door.

Lessa lingered on the bridge. "You coming?"

"You guys go on. I'll catch up with you later."

They needed the time to deal with Cade's death, time to absorb what had happened and grieve. Rion tried to find the words to explain her need for solitude, but Lessa—always gifted at reading others—simply stopped by her chair, put her hand on Rion's shoulder, and squeezed.

After the crew had disembarked and Ram Chalva had been taken by medical personnel to the hospital in New Tyne, Rion went to her quarters, slid into her desk chair, and ran her hands over her face. Her back was killing her again. She'd need medical attention herself soon . . . but some things couldn't wait. She exhaled deeply and then ripped the bandage off her past. If anything, it'd be a distraction from her grief. . . .

"You there, AI? Little Bit?"

"I am here."

"Mind if I call you that? Little Bit?"

"I do not mind that colloquial designation if it suits your purpose. I myself cannot remember my original designation."

"What happened to your facility?"

"Many things. Many things. Like many parts. My recollection is . . . spotty."

"Start with the *Spirit of Fire*."

"*The Reclaimers, yes. They came. Enemies to the Covenant. The Reclaimers destroyed the sphere. Why would they do such a thing? Why would you do such a thing?*"

"I didn't," Rion assured it. "Tell me about the Reclaimers."

"*They had an impressive AI on that ship, given their rudimentary technology of course. A little haughty for my tastes . . . She was quick, and her calculations were very well composed. They destroyed the sphere, destroyed all of our beautiful ships. The* Spirit of Fire. *Aptly named, for that's all she brought to our sanctuary. Burned everything and blew parts of me and my directive straight out into the system.*"

"And the ship? What happened to the ship?"

"*It . . . One moment. Yes, you call it slingshot. It slung around our artificial sun and through the sphere. Left the system. They wouldn't have gotten far.*"

"Why's that?"

"*Because they used their slipspace drive to trigger a supernova and destroy the sanctuary. They lost the ability to access and navigate slipspace.*"

Rion released a heavy breath. So they'd been truly lost. "Do you have any images or feeds relating to the Reclaimers?"

"*Some, yes from my feed at Relay 07756.*"

"Play on-screen, will you?"

A slide show of scenes began to appear, most of them grainy and distant, showing Sangheili and even a lofty-looking San'Shyuum. But they were just fragments, disjointed images that only told her the players, not the outcome.

Then, startlingly, her father's image appeared.

Rion jerked as if shocked. Everything inside her stilled, as if moving or breathing might make the image fade. It was him. Her dad. Looking into a camera lens and pointing. He appeared to be smiling and in the middle of saying something.

"How did you get this?"

"It was a simple matter to slip into their communications."

"Do you have audio?"

Static buzzed through the speakers on Rion's display. And then she heard it; his voice as he leaned close to a camera. *"Keep the coffee hot. I'll be back before you know it."*

Tears blurred her vision. The image cut off, replaced by a chaotic battle scene. It took her a moment to understand what she was now seeing. "Are those . . . ?"

"I believe you call them Spartans. The Reclaimers referred to them as Red Team."

On the vid feed, three Spartans were taking on a group of Sangheili in close-quarter combat. At the bottom edge of the screen, Rion saw her father, going in and out of frame, as he too fought like hell.

The feed suddenly gave way to lines of static and Rion shot to her feet, ignoring the stab of pain in her back. "Wait, what happened?"

"At the time this was chronicled, I began moving critical systems and making copies of myself and sending them to every station on the sphere. They were going to destroy the sphere."

"You keep saying 'sphere.' You mean the planet, right?"

"No, it was but a construct, a sanctuary. A large artificial refuge, if you will."

"Pull up the shot before the battle, the one with the audio." The AI complied. "Freeze-frame."

Again, it was him. John Forge. Her heart pounded slow and hard, and she felt a little sick as she slid back into her chair.

"Were you able to track the *Spirit of Fire* before the sphere blew?"

"I only have its initial trajectory."

They would have all gone into cryo. Unless they found a planet, established a base camp, waited for rescue. . . .

"Scan this and nearby systems. Create a map and highlight planets or moons capable of supporting human life based on their trajectory. Also, can you tell me if there were any human casualties during the Reclaimer's fight with the Covenant?"

"I'm sorry, I do not possess that information. Map complete, Captain."

Rion sat back, amazed by the speed at which the AI worked, and studied the star map as it appeared, with systems and planets highlighted as possible destinations for the ship. The idea that she might be looking at the *Spirit of Fire*'s final home made her release a disbelieving laugh.

"Captain? I really don't believe you understand the definition of 'humorous,' as I stated earlier. Shall I explain it again?"

"No, thank you. I need you to communicate with Doctor Martoli in New Tyne. Tell him I need an appointment. Today."

"Of course. I'll inquire now. Also, we should discuss your engineer. . . ."

"Not now," she said tiredly, staring at the map and feeling like the odds were stacked against her. Maybe they always had been. Following that map required another leap of faith.

Another shot in the dark. Another risk.

Her gaze settled on the wall beyond the screen. On it was a painting Lessa had done during her first long-distance flight as an official crewmember. There were also photographs. Lessa and Niko on Sundown six months ago. A candid one of Cade during the same trip, looking over his shoulder, the sparkling blue water of the resort pool behind him, that wicked grin of his . . .

He always called her lucky. Always with the shake of his head and a smile.

Her heart tightened so hard and quick it left her gasping for air. She tore her gaze from the wall.

Her lucky streak had cost Cade his life.

Now he was gone.

He'd made her think of possibilities, of a different life, a settled one. She could still have that. It wasn't too late.

Yet those things seemed like a dream now. They were in direct opposition to her livelihood, her ongoing quest to find her father . . . and now her burning need to make Gek 'Lhar pay.

She wanted to rip those dog tags from the hinge-head's shoulder and watch the light die in his one good eye.

Losing Cade made her feel reckless and volatile with very little thought to her own preservation. But the opposite was true when it came to her crew. She had to be more cautious now, more aware of her responsibilities to them, more determined to keep them safe.

They were, after all, her family.

The Forerunner artifacts orbiting the dwarf star held a treasure trove of salvage, a site that would feed the *Ace of Spades*'s crew over several lifetimes. With the money, Lessa and Niko could live out any dream they ever had, purchase a house, go to school—*own* a school, for that matter. Kip could collect every ship he'd ever studied. Hell, he could buy a whole damn fleet if he wanted. The options were endless.

They could have an amazing life.

And that posed a problem. Because Rion wanted that for them . . . but she also wanted more.

She drummed her fingers on the table, eyeing the images on the wall and the star map in front of her.

The salvage was out there.

Cade's killer was out there.

Her father and the *Spirit of Fire* were out there.

She just had to decide where to start. . . .

ACKNOWLEDGMENTS

My deepest thanks to Ed Schlesinger, Frank O'Connor, Jeremy Patenaude, Tiffany O'Brien, Sparth, and the entire team at 343. Gratitude also goes to my agent, Miriam Kriss; my family: Jonathan, Audrey, and James; my sister, Kameryn Long, for the help; and to Army veteran John Burt for sharing his time and knowledge.

ABOUT THE AUTHOR

KELLY GAY is the critically acclaimed author of the Charlie Madigan urban fantasy series. She is a multipublished author with works translated into several languages. She is a two-time RITA nominee, an ARRA nominee, a Goodreads Choice Awards finalist, and a SIBA Book Award Long List finalist. Kelly is also a recipient of the North Carolina Arts Council's Fellowship Grant in Literature. She can be found online at KellyGay.com.